The Flying Ace

The Adventures of Silver Dove, Book Eight

Eliza Scalia

Cover Illustration by: Wayne F. Shurtz and
Cheyanne and Jean Buffkin
Based upon the characters originally
designed by Suji Gallianetti

Copyright © **2021 Eliza Scalia**

Published by: Winged Publications

ISBN: 978-1-956654-14-1

Dedicated to my friend who, earlier this year, decided that life was not worth living anymore. You were always a great support for my writing and encouraged me to be better with it. I wish that things could have been different for us and that you were still here. I miss you.

Chapter One
Colomba-
Bright Morning,
Dark Thoughts

The bus glides across the road as the morning sun shines through the windows. As we all make our way to school, Nat, Luis, and I are sitting on the fake leather seats chatting about anything and everything, simply just enjoying each other's company. I try to keep my mind locked in on what they are saying, but my ears keep picking up some of the conversations around me, and a lot of them aren't very nice. I keep hearing people talking badly about Silver Dove (AKA me), whispering to each other hatefully that I will lose to the Crow one day and that I am weak since I haven't defeated him completely yet even though he has been in our school almost two years now. Silver Dove and the Crow have become the school's main thing to gossip about and it makes me squirm every time I hear a new rumor about us starting. Some of them are funny (like when someone said that the Crow is an evil robot while I am a magical fairy sent by

Heaven to protect everyone, that one made me laugh so hard I couldn't breathe for a minute), while others have been mean (like when they talk about how the Crow will kill me one day and take over the world, that one made me want to curl in a ball and cry for a few hours).

My heart feels as if it has fallen into my stomach. I know that I haven't done the best as Silver Dove, but I have saved this school from all of the people the Crow has transformed, haven't I? Shouldn't I get some credit for that? When I listen to the people around me though, I can tell that they don't think I should. They are putting all the blame on me even though I think that they should be blaming themselves. I mean, the Crow says that he's here to stop all the bullying, but they keep doing it anyway even after I have stopped so many of these bullied kids that the Crow has transformed. I keep telling myself that, but I still feel terrible knowing that all these people I've been protecting are thinking such horrible things about me even though I have tried so hard to save them. I suppose that there is no way to please them, they will never be satisfied.

"What about you, Colomba?" I jump a little in surprise in my seat. I was so wrapped in my own thoughts that I forgot I was part of a conversation with Nat and Luis.

"I'm sorry Nat, what were you saying?" Nat grins at me. She can obviously tell that my mind was elsewhere, but she doesn't let that bother herself as she repeats her question to me.

"I was asking if you have a Valentine for

tomorrow that you've been hiding from us?" I feel my face burning and I know that I am blushing. My mind flashes back to a few events that have happened over the past few days. Several guys I know, and one or two that I don't know, have asked me to be their Valentine. They were all very sweet, one boy even gave me some chocolates when he asked, but I turned them all down. I couldn't say yes to any of them because I do not care for them the same way as they do for me. I couldn't say yes because that would just be lying to them, and I could never play with a boy's feelings like that. I would feel like a monster if I did. I could never hurt anybody like that. I know that most girls my age have already had a boyfriend or two before, but I haven't. I've been wanting to focus more on school so that I can follow my dreams and get into a good college and be a doctor, boys would get in the way of that. Maybe I am a bit weird, but at least I am going after what I want in life. That's something isn't it? That makes it not so bad, right? Also, I've just never found a guy that I want to be with. I have to hold back a sigh at that thought. I have never even had a crush before. I am definitely weird for a girl my age.

I glance back up to see that Nat and Luis are looking at me. It takes me a moment to realize that they are waiting for me to answer Nat's question. I was so wrapped up in my own thoughts that I completely forgot about it.

"No, no I don't have a Valentine. I don't think I will by the time Valentine's Day arrives. I guess it will be just like any other day for me." Nat seems a bit disappointed by that, while Luis almost seems happy about it. That's weird.

As I look away from them so I can grab my lip balm out of my backpack, from the corner of my eye I notice that Nat gives Luis a strange look. It almost looks like she is upset with him and is trying to convince him to do something. Luis just looks at her with a guilty face, smiling awkwardly at her. What on earth is all that about?

When I look back up at them, their strange expressions are gone, and they are back to normal. I don't bother to ask them what all that was about, I know that they would just pretend to not know what I'm talking about. Oh well, I'll let them have their little secret.

The bus pulls up in front of the school so that the three of us can start another day.

Chapter Two
Luis-
My Valentine

The entire school seems to be filled with heart shaped decorations and streamers of pink and red. Valentine's Day used to just make me feel angry and lonely because I was always stuck by myself without having anybody to share the holiday with. It is different this time though. Now I have someone that I want to be my Valentine. Colomba is walking beside me, wearing a white dress with little pink hearts. Even though it is the day before Valentine's Day, she apparently still wanted to dress up for it.

I always thought of Valentine's Day as a dumb holiday, probably because I didn't have a girlfriend then. At the moment though, I'm kind of looking forward to it. Although I do feel a bit queasy because of how nervous I am. Tomorrow is going to be the day, I'm going to tell Colomba how I feel about her.

I have been putting it off for almost two years now. I have no more excuses, I will tell her. I should have told her years ago, but I kept telling myself that I was too weak, that I should wait until I have ended all the bullying so that she wouldn't see me as such a complete loser. I know now that she doesn't really care about that, she cares about me as I am. She may only care about me as a friend right now, but I hope that once she sees how much I care about her then she might see me in a different way. I am also a lot stronger than I was before. It's not as if I have been working out or anything, but I mean that I'm stronger on the inside. Being the Crow has probably been the best thing that has ever happened to me. It has helped me find the strength that has been hidden in me for so long. Now I just need to show that strength to the world, to show it to Colomba.

After Colomba told Nat and I on the bus that she doesn't have a Valentine for tomorrow, I will admit I felt really good. It's nice to know that she hasn't accepted anybody else, I still have a chance. Nat had looked at me with frustration as soon as Colomba's back was turned. She knows how I feel about Colomba and wants me to tell her, but I couldn't do it then. I need to make it the perfect moment. I want it to be perfect, just for her, is that wrong?

As the two of us head to our first classes, a familiar face instantly creates a fire that burns in my blood, Alex. He is leaning against some lockers as he talks to some of his football team buddies. As one of his friends talks, Alex's eyes wander a bit before they stop dead on Colomba. When his eyes lock on her, a sinister grin crawls across his face. The look in his eyes as he looks at her is almost like the gaze of a lion looking at a zebra, as if he is the hunter and she is his prey. I want to march over to him and punch him through the teeth for daring to look at her like that, doesn't he have any respect? Why am I asking this? I know that he has no respect for anyone, not even the girl he has had a crush on ever since we all started high school. I may love Colomba, but so does he. His love isn't true like mine though, he just likes her since she is beautiful, I can just tell from the way he looks at her. My blood boils whenever I see him looking at her like this.

My heart jumps a little in my chest as he continues looking at her and I realize something obvious, he's probably going to ask her to be his Valentine too. She has been acting friendly towards him too. I can only hope and pray that when he does ask, she says no.

Alex's eyes leave her for a moment to finally notice that she is not alone. His eyes narrow when he sees me, his eyes burning with fury. In his gaze I can clearly see the message he is trying to send. The two of us are in competition for her, and he will do anything to win her heart. I glare back at him, sending the same message right back to him. I will do anything to win her heart.

Chapter Three
Colomba-
Lexi

First period ends and everyone rushes into the hall to meet up with friends so they can walk together to their next class. I leave my class with a smile on my face, eager to see my friends. As I look around though I notice something different today about the crowd around me. All around me, people are paired off into couples who lovingly hold each other's hands or hold each other close as they walk together. Everyone is in a couple except me, I stand all alone. The smile disappears as I see this, my cheerful heart suddenly feeling a bit lonely. I almost never feel lonely since I always have friends here at school and my dad and grandma at home, but today just feels different. Tomorrow is Valentine's Day, the day we celebrate love, but when you don't have someone to love like that, it can be a very lonely day. Suddenly, that loneliness disappears when a familiar voice calls out my name behind me. I turn around with the smile back on my face to see Luis waving at me, he runs over to meet me with Nat following him. It only takes him a minute to reach me, and he smiles down at me with his warm, gentle smile.

"Hey Colomba how's it going?" Nat catches up to us, breathing deeply from her run, and the three of us start walking together.

"I'm doing well, just enjoying all the decorations." I point above us where someone had put red, pink, and white streamers as decorations for Valentine's Day. "It all looks so great." Even though I was feeling a little sad a moment ago because of the holiday, I have to admit that the decorations all over the school are fantastic. The streamers are spread everywhere along the ceiling, large decorated red hearts are on each door, and little pictures of Cupid are all over the place. Nat grins up at the decorations like a little kid smiling in a candy store. Valentine's Day has always been her favorite holiday. She's one of those girls who loves romance so having a holiday just for that is great for her.

"Yeah, apparently a girl named Lexi did all of this." Nat says, obviously just as impressed as I am by this girl's awesome decorating skills. "Apparently nobody else wanted to help her so she did it all on her own."

"You've got to be kidding me." I say, completely stunned.

"I know right? It's amazing that anybody can do this alone." It is amazing, but that wasn't why I was so surprised. Why didn't anybody else want to help her? How could they leave her by herself to do such a big job? If I had known that they would be decorating, I would have helped her. Knowing that she did all this by herself, I really wish I did know, I would have helped her no matter how long it took.

Glancing down the hall, I can see that, apparently, the decorating isn't quite done yet. A girl is standing on top of a ladder, putting some streamers across the ceiling. A cardboard box of more decorations sits on top of the ladder with her. She moves the streamers out from in front of her face so that I can see that it is the girl Nat had been talking about, Lexi. I'm not good friends with her, but I do know who she is. From what I have heard she is a very kind person and will do anything to make someone smile. My smile fades a bit when I remember something else I have heard about her, she gets bullied a lot. Other people pick on her because they say that she's ugly. I don't see that though.

Her face is thin and her skin is a permanent tan-ish color since her family is from the Philippines. Dark eyes stare at the streamers she is putting up. Her pin straight hair falls down to the middle of her back. Lexi may not be beautiful, but she's not ugly, she is just... average. The one characteristic she has that people make fun of her for, and say that she's ugly for it, are her ears. Since her hair is so straight and falls so close to her face, you can easily see that her ears stick out more than most people's. I barely even notice this, but everyone else seems to think that this is a big deal. I honestly don't get it.

I move a little faster toward her, I want to ask her if she would like some help. Something stops me in my tracks though, a feeling. Since I have the

Silver Dove Pin, whenever something bad is about to happen I get this feeling to warn me. Now that feeling is trying to warn me, but when I look around, I don't see anything unusual. My eyes spot Angela Turner, the snobby brat of our school, walk close to Lexi's ladder. Before I can do anything to help, Lexi accidently bumps the box of decorations with her elbow, and it falls off the ladder and right on top of Angela. The box lands so that the open side falls on Angela and gets stuck on her head. Streamers rain down from the fallen box and the bundle of streamers tumble around on the ground, spreading the colorful paper all over. The hallway breaks into a roar of laughter, but I stay silent, fearful for what I know will happen.

Angela rips the box off her head and glares up at Lexi with so much fury that Lexi shivers at the top of the ladder. Even though I am around ten feet away from them, I still shudder at the sight of Angela's anger. I know from personal experience how frightening she can be when that anger is directed at you.

"What was that for, you ugly little freak?!" The entire hallway stops laughing at the sound of the cold hatred in Angela's voice. Lexi moves down the ladder slowly, I can see her hands quivering on the rungs of the ladder in her terror.

"I- I'm sorry." Lexi practically whispers this as she gets off the ladder. She is practically cowering in fear, as if she expects Angela to hit her. Which I doubt will happen but with the anger in her eyes, I wouldn't be surprised if Angela tries though. I try to move through the crowd to get to them, to try and help Lexi, but the crowd just seems to get thicker by the moment, making it almost impossible to move between everyone.

"Sorry!?" Angela practically roars at her. *"Sorry is all you can say!? You have got to be kidding me! Why are you even putting up these stupid decorations anyway? It's not like anyone is going to want to be your Valentine, you're just going to be alone just like all the other ugly losers in this school! Face it, who's going to want to go out with an ugly girl with giant elephant ears!"*

Lexi's face immediately shows her hurt, tears spring up in her eyes before she runs away from Angela, racing down the hall through the crowd that creates a path for her. The crowd realizes that the show is over, and everyone starts heading to their next classes while I stay still, completely devastated that I couldn't help her. Someone places their hand gently on my shoulder, I turn around to see Nat smiling at me comfortingly, she obviously knows that I was trying to help her but couldn't and knows that I am upset by this.

"Don't worry about this, Lexi will get over it and Angela will just go on and pick on someone else in about ten minutes. Besides, Angela just said that since nobody would ever want to be her Valentine. Just image being Angela's Valentine, that sounds like a nightmare come true." Even though I just saw something pretty sad, I have to hold back a laugh at what Nat just said. Somehow she always makes me laugh, even when I feel like I may cry. Luis appears at my other side, and he smiles softly down at me. He can also see how sad I am about what happened.

"C'mon Colomba, let's get out of here. Maybe we will see Lexi later and we can help her then." I smile up at him, suddenly feeling a lot better.

"Okay, let's go." As we pass by the ladder Lexi had been standing on, we pick up the box she had dropped on Angela and quickly get everything that had fallen out back in the box before setting it against the wall so that nobody will trip over it. The three of us walk to class, Nat and Luis are smiling joyfully, while my smile is fake.

Earlier today, I was upset when I heard some people saying that I was weak as Silver Dove since I haven't stopped the Crow yet. I tried to defend myself in my mind, but now I see their point. He is trying to end the bullying so I'm trying to stop it whenever I see it, but I can't even do that right. I can't even defend one girl from Angela. Actually, there have been many times when I couldn't do anything when somebody was getting bullied right in front of me, and when I did try something bad happened afterwards.

Maybe I am a complete failure as Silver Dove. Maybe everyone is right, and I will lose to the Crow one day. Maybe there is no point in trying anymore. Maybe I should just give up. While everyone in the hallway chats happily with their friends around them, I feel as if my entire world is falling apart and I am powerless to fix it.

Chapter Four
Luis-
Cards in the
Locker

The bell rings signaling the end of class, it blares loudly and everyone gets up from their desk to head out into the hallway. While everyone else heads to their next class, I head to Colomba's locker. She always goes to her locker between these classes to trade out some of her books, I always meet her there every day so that we can walk together to our next class. It doesn't take me long to get there, and Colomba makes it to her locker only a moment after I arrive.

"Hey Luis, how's it going?" she asks with her usual cheerful grin. I smile back at her, staring straight into her perfect aquamarine eyes.

"Going great. Can't complain." As I lean against the locker next to hers, she manages to unlock it and pull her locker open, several colorful pieces of paper fall out as she does this. I bend over to pick them up for her when I realize what they are, Valentine's cards. I feel my face grow hot as a wave of anger goes through me. As Colomba puts some books in her locker, I quickly open a few of the cards to see that they are all from guys asking her to be their girlfriend. I want to crumple these cards up and throw them in the trash where they belong, but Colomba saw them fall out of the locker and she saw me pick them up, so I know that she would be hurt if I did do that. When her books are in her locker, I hand them to her, and she glances through them as if she isn't surprised by having so many guys asking her out. My heart sinks a little deeper into my chest and I suddenly feel sick as a depressing thought goes through my mind. When it comes to Colomba, I only really think of my competition with Alex for her, but there are probably many other guys in this school who have realized just how pretty, sweet, and all around awesome she is. They all probably want her to be their Valentine just like I do.

"Hey, umm…. Have you been getting a lot of those?" Colomba blushes softly as she places the cards back in her locker, trying not to look into my eyes.

"I've gotten a few." I notice another set of cards that are placed on top of a few books. With those, plus the ones that just fell out of her locker, I would suspect that there are around ten Valentine's cards. I cross my arms as I feel my hands tighten into fists.

"It looks like there were more than a few. You seem to be pretty popular with the guys around here." Her blush grows even darker, making her entire face a light pink.

"Yeah, I guess so. It's kind of embarrassing and a little sad too. I feel bad that I will have to turn them down. I'm not looking forward to that at all." I feel my fists suddenly loosen their grip and my body relax.

"Really? You're going to turn all of them down?" She glances up at me, looking a bit confused.

"Of course, I don't really feel the same for any of them, and it would be wrong for me to say yes to a guy if I don't feel the same way. That would just be leading him on, and I could never do that." I look down at my shoes as I gather all my courage to ask her a question.

"Is there any guy that you are interested in?" Colomba glances down at her feet too, completely uncomfortable.

"No, nobody." She smiles up at me. "Don't worry, if I was interested in someone I would tell you, you're my best friend." Alright, that hurt, that wounded me. I just got friend zoned into a whole new dimension, dang. Wow my heart hurts right now. Colomba doesn't seem to notice that I am in pain though since she still smiles as she places one last book in her locker. I open my mouth to say something to her, to possibly be a man for once and tell her that one more guy likes her that she might be interested in, but I am interrupted. Someone comes up from behind Colomba's locker door and closes it so that they can have her full attention. I'm not surprised when I see that the person who closed the locker is Alex, a superior smirk on his face.

"Hey there beautiful, how are you doing?"

Colomba looks a bit annoyed that he closed the door on her.

"I'm fine Alex." She picks up her bag and Alex notices something next to her foot. He picks it up to find that one of the Valentine's Day cards must have fallen out of her locker when he had closed it. Alex doesn't even have any shame with this, he opens it up and reads it out loud, using a mocking voice as if he is joking around, but his face shows his anger.

"Hi Colomba, I have always thought you were the prettiest girl I have ever seen." Colomba glares at him as he mocks whoever wrote her the Valentine. He just ignores this as he keeps reading. "I was hoping that for Valentine's Day we could see each other after school at the Captain's Ship Diner. Love, Derek." Alex laughs as he tosses the Valentine to the ground. Colomba quickly picks the card back up, her eyes hurt as she looks up at Alex who is still laughing at the poor guy who wrote the Valentine.

"Please tell me that you aren't actually going to go out with a loser like that." Even though he is chuckling as he says this, I can see the fire of jealousy hiding behind his eyes. I want to laugh at how pathetic he is by getting so jealous over a card, but then I remember that I was getting mad over the same thing just a minute ago. That makes me shut up instantly. Colomba's face turns crimson from both anger and embarrassment as she places the Valentine's card inside one of her books.

"No, I don't plan on it. I'm not interested in him like that." Alex seems to become more calm after this and he smiles at her in a way that reminds me of a wolf staring at a piece of meat. It's almost as if he is hunting her and he knows he can get her.

"Well that's good, because I know someone much better who would love to take you out for a good time tomorrow." The look he's giving her right now makes my blood boil. I want hit him across the face with the large book that Colomba is holding. "How 'bout it? You have any plans for after school tomorrow?" Colomba just looks at him with a blank expression for a moment before giving him an answer.

"No." And she walks away without another word. I have to hold back laughter as Alex watches her retreating figure with a look of absolute shock. I have to practically run after Colomba to make sure I don't laugh in front of him. To laugh at Alex after he gets rejected by a girl would be an instant death sentence, and I'm having way too much fun right now to die. I catch up to Colomba and I walk beside her as we head to class. She still looks a little annoyed, so I nudge her shoulder with my arm. When she looks up at me, I give her a teasing grin and this instantly makes her smile.

"Don't get annoyed by him Colomba, he doesn't deserve any of your emotions." Especially your love. I want to add that little bit as well, but my stomach instantly turns into knots at the thought of saying it out loud. She casts her eyes down.

"Yeah, I know, he just really gets under my skin most of the time."

"Then why do you put up with him so much? Why don't you just tell him to back off? I've seen you do it before." She looks into my eyes with almost a guilty look.

"I guess I just feel bad for him, and I don't want to hurt his feelings by telling him to go away. I don't think he's a very happy person and I don't think he has a lot of real friends." I don't say anything, but I know what she's talking about. I know that she probably knows about how Alex does not have a good life at home. His dad is extremely mean to him. I realized that after a football game when I had transformed Alex into the Bull-Y. I saw how Alex's dad spoke to him, and I know that he's probably worse when they are in the privacy of their home. I can only imagine what life is like for him when he is at his house. Colomba probably saw that too, or she has figured it out somehow. Either way she pities him, and it kind of makes me feel good to know that she pities this guy that I hate… Well, that sounded really mean, I really need to rethink things in my life. Colomba shrugs her shoulders, looking a bit defeated. "I guess that I just want to make him feel like he has one real friend here, but then he just does something annoying like that and I snap at him." The guilt instantly returns in her eyes. "I feel terrible whenever I do that, but sometimes I just feel so angry that it just comes out." She sighs softly. "I don't really know what to do, but I can't just abandon him like that, I couldn't hurt him like that." I clear my throat, trying to figure out what to say.

"Well… maybe you should just focus on what's best for you. If he's bothering you, that's his choice, it's not because of anything else at all. It's just his choice. You don't have to let him do this to you if you don't like it. Let him bother someone else. You deserve better." Colomba smiles at me, but there is still a trace of sadness in her eyes.

"Thanks Luis, don't worry about me though. I'll get through it." I try to smile back at her, but it feels pretty fake. I hate seeing this happen to her, she deserves to be treated better than she does by that creep. She is a lady, and a lady needs a gentleman in her life. Even though that's how I feel, I know that I can't just tell her what to do, I need to respect her choice.

"Okay, I get it. I hope it works out for you. If you ever need any help, you know that I'm here and I'll do anything to help you. You know that right?" Her smile is sincere now.

"Of course I know that, you're one of the greatest friends I've ever had. I know I can trust you with anything." She gives me a tight hug which I eagerly return. Even though I am happy with my arms around her like this, I still feel a bit sad by her words. I am just her friend. Maybe I am just kidding myself when I say that she may say yes if I do ask her out for Valentine's Day. As I look down at her beautiful face, and intelligent bright eyes, I know that she could do so much better than me. She is out of my league. A guy like me can only just be a friend to a girl like her.

The two of us end our embrace and we walk beside each other on our way to class, but to me it feels like we are miles apart.

Chapter Five
Colomba-
Ace

I walk down the hall feeling a bit melancholy. As the crowd of people walks around me, I can only think of two people, Alex and Luis. I think about what Luis said, about how I deserve better than what Alex has been doing to me and that I shouldn't have to deal with him and his obnoxious behavior. When I start thinking about how right he is, I then think about Alex and everything he has to go through. His father seems like he's a monster to him at home, I can only hope that he isn't as bad as I fear. When I think about no longer talking to him, I feel guilty because I know that he may be losing the only person who hangs out with him just to be with him, not to hang out with him since he's the star player of the school sports teams or because he is popular. Also, he has never been truly unkind to me, just obnoxious, to be unkind to someone who has kind to you is just wrong. I may not want his company, but I can't do something that I think is wrong. What would that make me if I did that even though I thought of it as wrong? I already know the answer to that question though, it would make me a monster. I would be hurting someone who has never hurt me.

My thoughts are interrupted when I glance through the crowd and see a familiar face. It is that girl that I saw getting hurt by Angela earlier today, Lexi. She is walking through the crowd, her eyes glazed over with misery, as if she is thinking about a really sad memory. Her shoulders are caved in around herself and her head is down, as if she is trying to hide from the world. With her body in that position, she almost reminds me of Luis whenever I see him walking down the hall alone. Despite how tall he is, he always appears so small whenever he is like that, as if the world is trying to make him disappear. That image quickly leaves my mind when someone opens their locker door very suddenly in front of Lexi, too fast for her to get out of the way. Her face smacks into the locker and she lets out a yelp of pain that makes the entire hall fall silent before breaking up into laughter as Lexi rubs her face in pain. The guy who had opened his locker chuckles along with the crowd.

"Sorry about that Elephant Ears, I just thought that with ears like those you would just be able to fly out of the way. You could be quite the flying ace that way." This gets the entire hallway to start laughing at Lexi again. She looks around at all the laughing faces around her, tears quickly fill her eyes before she runs off crying down the hall. I push through the crowd to follow after her, not even caring if I insult anybody by doing this, I just follow after Lexi as she uses one of the exits to enter the school courtyard. The courtyard is simply a small area of grass and sidewalks that lead to different doors that can take you to different parts of the school. Flowerbeds line around the school, lovingly taken care of by Rosie, a girl that the Crow transformed into the Black Iris last year. This is a peaceful place, usually a quiet place if it wasn't for the sound of soft sobbing. I look around a corner to find Lexi sitting on a bench with her head in her hands, her shoulders are shaking as I hear her taking in deep, uneven breaths. She is obviously crying.

I rush over and sit on the bench beside her, too worried about her to even think that she may want to be alone.

"Lexi, I saw what happened, are you alright? Does your head still hurt?" She lifts her head suddenly, her eyes wide in fright. She must not have noticed that I had been here. "Sorry, I didn't mean to scare you." She sniffles softly as she turns away from me to stare ahead at some flowers across the sidewalk from us.

"Shouldn't you be the one afraid of me, everyone else thinks I look like a monster, so shouldn't you be running away from me?" I look into her eyes, trying to see if she's joking with me, but she's not.

"What on earth are you talking about? You don't look like a monster. You are just a regular person, just like me." She scoffs at me as if I said something amusing.

"Oh please, you heard what they said, you heard what they always call me. They think I look like a freak." She holds her hands over her ears, the ears that everyone makes fun of. "And they're right." I shake my head, feeling so frustrated with how everyone can mistreat her just because they think one part of her appearance doesn't look right.

"No, they're not. They are not right. There is nothing wrong with you at all." She shakes her head right back at me.

"Yes there is, if there wasn't they wouldn't make fun of me so much. I'm sorry you're too blind to see it." I suddenly embrace her, completely filled with pity for her. She does not hug me back, but she rests her head on my shoulder as she starts to cry again.

"I am not blind. I can see you, and you are alright, there is nothing wrong with you. You are perfectly fine just as you are." She shudders a little as she sobs for a moment before speaking again.

"I just wish everyone would love each other no matter what they looked like." I rub my hand against her back, trying to sooth her.

"I know what you mean, I wish for the same thing." I feel her body stiffen under my touch as soon as those words leave my lips. She practically pushes herself out of my grip to glare at me with pure venom shining in her eyes. I lean a little bit away from her, suddenly feeling a little afraid.

"How would you know?! Everyone loves you since you're so pretty! Everyone tries to stay away from me since I'm ugly because my ears stick out and make me look like a freak!" I feel my eyes grow wide at her words.

"Don't you dare say that about yourself. It

doesn't matter what they think. I think you're a beautiful person because you do so much just to make people happy. Just think about all the great decorations you have been putting up all over the school. You are a beautiful person on the inside and, honestly, I think you are pretty on the outside too. So what if you don't like one thing about yourself, you have plenty of other features that are fantastic. You have beautiful brown eyes, you have lovely hair. Why are you trying to look down on yourself for one thing when you have many other great features?" She laughs coldly at me as she stands up from the bench and looks down at me.

"Oh please, don't believe all those stupid fairy tales you read as a kid. What you look like does matter. Nobody will love you if you look ugly like me! Face it, the pretty girls like you always have it easy while the ugly ones like me have to just scrape by in life! Life is always worse for ugly people like me!" She runs back into the school with tears streaming down her face before I can say anything more. I sit alone for a second, stunned by what has just happened. Thankfully the warning bell rings, bringing me back to reality so that I can rush to my next class. I make it just in time, the bell ringing just as I entered the room. I sit down at my desk, a little out of breath from the run. I have to force Lexi out of my mind as the teacher starts class. Even though the lesson they are teaching is interesting, I find that Lexi keeps popping into my mind, her sad words repeating themselves over and over again. Her hatred for herself just seems to burn a hole in my soul, frightened at the idea of having thoughts like that for myself. My life has been good, and I try to think well about myself, so it makes my heart break hearing someone speak so badly about themselves. I can only hope that she can see how foolish she is being and that she can start looking at herself in a more positive light someday soon. Judging from how she was talking though, that will probably take a very long time.

Chapter Six
Luis-
What Is Said

Lexi marches right past me in rage, not even noticing me hiding in a corner in the courtyard, just like I had hoped. I didn't want her to realize that I had seen everything that had happened. I have always felt invisible in this world, and I have always felt angry about that, but every now and again it comes in handy like when I am doing some work as the Crow. Just like now.

After what I just saw them do to Lexi, I'm thinking that it's time for me to return as the Crow. If they can show that much cruelty to someone who hasn't done anything and is always nice, then the other people in this school deserve to be punished.

I think back on some of the things that Lexi said, my heart aching for her. She was right about a lot. The people who aren't good looking in this world have a much harder time in life. I glance at my reflection on a window, people like me. I've always had to struggle just to make it through life. All the other people in school thought I was ugly, and no girl would ever look my way, until I met one. I look over at that one now, Colomba. As I stare at her beautiful, sweet face, I can't help but think about another thing that Lexi said. She said that she wished that people would love each other no matter how they looked. When I look at Colomba, I wish for the same thing. I wish she could love me even though I'm an ugly, pathetic loser. When I look at her though, I know that she would never go out with someone like me. I will always be trapped in her friendship, never a boyfriend.

Even though I have all this power as the Crow, I still don't have the power to make her love me the way I want her to. I can't make her fall into my arms, begging me to be her boyfriend. Life doesn't work like that, especially not for a guy like me. Honestly, I would give away all of my powers if I could just do that, if I could just make her love me. I would be happy forever if I could do that.

Colomba hears the warning bell for our next class and runs out of the courtyard and back into school while I run the other way. I run through the door and head to class, making it just in time before the bell rings. I sit down as the teacher starts class, but my heart isn't really in it, my mind is too busy thinking about Lexi and her problems. Most of my thoughts though are given to Colomba and how much I wish I could spend tomorrow, Valentine's Day, with her.

Chapter Seven
Colomba-
Valentine's Day

As I step into the kitchen at my house in the morning, I can see my grandmother already getting breakfast ready. She is in front of the stove with a frying pan in her hand.

"Good morning Nonna. How are you?" She turns around for a moment to give me a warm smile.

"Good morning Tesoro, I am doing wonderful. Happy Valentine's Day." I sit down at the table as she brings over a plate for me with the frying pan in the other hand. She sets the plate down and carefully slides my breakfast onto my plate. I have to laugh when I see that she made heart shaped pancakes for breakfast.

"You are super festive today." She laughs as well.

"Of course, do you have a special someone to spend the day with?" I look away from her, my smile fading a bit.

"No, not really." Her smile fades too.

"How is it possible that the people in your school are so blind that they cannot see a sweet, smart, beautiful girl like you and not want to be with you?" My smile returns, I think it's impossible not to smile when a grandma compliments you. Grandmas just have a special quality about them that just makes everything better, even when you are feeling sad.

"I guess I just haven't found the right guy that I want to date. There's not really anybody that I can see myself dating. A few guys asked me out, but I said no. I didn't really like any of them that way and I couldn't lie to them." I look down at the heart shaped pancake on the plate in front of me. "Maybe I'm just too picky or something or I focus too much on school and my duty as Silver Dove." Nonna surprises me by looking down at me with annoyance and placing her hands on her hips.

"And what is wrong with that?" My eyes open wide with surprise at her angry tone. "Knowing you, you would have realistic and very good expectations for the man you will be with, so you should not lower your expectations just to have a man in your life. You are too good for that. And when it comes to you focusing "too much" on your studies and your training as Silver Dove, that is ridiculous. You are spending time making yourself better and following your destiny. If a man does not recognize this and does not treat your dreams and duties with respect, then he is not worth your time. You are worthy of love and respect, do not forget that ever." I smile up at my grandmother as the tears threaten to fall down my face.

"Thank you." Nonna's angry expression fades swiftly as she realizes that her message has sunken in.

"You're welcome Tesoro." She sits down beside me and takes my hand in hers. "I know that everyone expects a girl your age to be with someone and that if you are not with someone then there must be something wrong with you, but there isn't. People might say otherwise, but there is nothing wrong with being alone, it just means that you haven't found the right person yet. That is alright, you are still young and have time. If a person thinks that they can never be alone, that shows that there is something wrong with them, not with you. Listen to the wisdom of an old woman, I have seen a great deal and have learned a lot. Learn to be happy with yourself before you welcome someone special into your life." I squeeze her hand in mine as I give her the warmest smile I can.

"I will." The two of us smile at each other before we both start eating breakfast, talking about more lighthearted things. Before I knew it, it was time to head out to the bus to head to school. I get on the bus to find Nat sitting by herself, Luis is nowhere to be seen.

"Hey Nat, where is Luis?" Nat shrugs at me.

"No idea, I haven't heard from him so I'm not sure if he is sick or not. I was hoping that he would be here since it's Valentine's Day, I was hoping that he would finally have the guts to tell you how he feels." Nat says this completely serious, and it annoys me.

"C'mon Nat, don't start that again. You've

been saying that forever, Luis is just a friend. You haven't said that in a while, I thought you had finally given up on that craziness." Nat just rolls her eyes at me.

"Yeah, yeah, believe what you want Birdy. He loves you and one day I hope he can finally admit it to you. I was just hoping that would be today." She lays her head back so that her braids fall down across the back of the bus seat. Nat closes her eyes in peace, looking very proud of herself for saying that. I know that she wants me to continue this conversation, but I won't give her that, I just remain silent. I don't need to deal with this today. I just want this day to go by peacefully. Everyone else can spend the holiday thinking about love, but not me, I will do what I need to do, focus on school and then go home. I just need to survive today.

Chapter Eight
Luis-
Valentine's Morning

I hop out of my Uncle Diego's car, give him a quick goodbye, and then rush inside the front doors of the school. I couldn't go on the bus this morning since I needed to get something before school started and I needed to go in a store to get it. I hold that item in my hand, a single star gazer lily. I wanted to get it this morning to make absolutely sure that it would be fresh, a wonderful girl should only be given the best flower. A girl like Colomba deserves the best.

I practically run through the halls to try and find Colomba before the first bell rings, starting classes. I have to do this before I lose my nerve. I promised myself the other day that today would be the day that I tell her how I truly feel, I will not let myself break that promise. It doesn't take me long to find her, she is standing by her open locker, pulling a few books out of her bag to put in her locker. I walk over to her casually, trying to look like I wasn't sprinting down the hall only moments ago to see her. I lean against the locker beside hers, trying to look relaxed when I really feel like I'm going to throw up in my nervousness.

"Hey Colomba, how's it going?" Wow she looks so beautiful today. She's wearing a white sweater with a pink skirt that has little white hearts on it. She has her hair pulled back in a ponytail with a matching pink ribbon with white hearts. She is so adorable. Colomba smiles at me with her usual warmth.

"It's going well for me. What's up with you?" My hand is sweating on the stem of the flower I'm holding behind my back.

"Not much, I just… um… I just…"

"Hey Colomba!" A confident voice shouts out from behind me. I turn around and groan softly when I see Alex coming toward us. He smiles at Colomba with confidence like I wish I could. He walks toward her, he doesn't even glance at me, it's almost as if I don't exist. I guess, to him, I don't exist unless he wants someone around to humiliate. Alex leans against the locker on Colomba's other side, he also has one of his hands behind his back for some reason.

"How're you doing beautiful?" Colomba smiles at him, but this smile doesn't have any warmth in it.

"Hey Alex. How are you?" She pulls a book out of her locker and closes it.

"I'm doing fantastic! How could I feel bad when I'm talking to the hottest girl in school?" Colomba glances away from his smiling face in embarrassment and a deep blush spreads across her cheeks. I can tell that she's pretty uncomfortable by his compliment, but I don't think he cares since he just keeps talking.

"I was hoping to run into you this morning because I didn't want to carry this around all day." From behind his back, he pulls out a huge bouquet of red roses. There must be around two dozen of them. Just from looking at the flowers, I can easily see that they are expensive. Colomba looks at the roses in surprise.

"Oh… thank you Alex. I-"

"I was hoping you would like them!" Alex interrupts. He holds the flowers out to Colomba, but she takes a step back from them.

"Yes, I do like them Alex, but I-"

"Yeah, I really wanted to give these to you today since-" he tries to hand the flowers to her, but she takes another step back.

"I understand Alex, but-"

"I wanted to ask you something. Would you like to go out-" Colomba interrupts him with a fit of sneezing that instantly silences him. She sneezes a couple of times before she is able to speak.

"Alex, I'm allergic to roses!" Alex quickly pulls the roses away from her, looking disappointed. Colomba sniffles a little and I give her a tissue from my backpack.

"Thanks Luis." She smiles at me as she dabs at her watery eyes with the tissue. "Sorry guys, but I'm going to have to go to the bathroom to throw some cold water on my eyes. Thanks for the roses Alex, but I'm afraid that I can't accept them. I'll see you guys later." She walks away from the two of us, still sniffling. I silently smirk at him, and his hands tighten around the flowers so forcefully in his anger that his knuckles turn white. I quickly walk away before he can do anything. As I walk to my locker, I chuckle to myself. Wow he's an idiot. Alex has been chasing after Colomba for almost two years now, but he didn't even know that she's allergic to roses? That's pathetic. If you want to be with a girl then you should at least try to know her a little, especially to know what she's allergic to. I guess this just shows what I've always thought, he only really likes her because she's pretty. He doesn't really care about her as a person, he doesn't care enough to know the real her. When I make it to my locker, I place the lily in there. I stare at it for a moment and the smile disappears from my face.

I could only afford this one flower to give her while Alex could buy two dozen roses. I bet that when he bought those, he didn't even have to worry about how much it cost. His family is loaded, so he probably doesn't have a care in the world when it comes to money. Colomba deserves to be given nice things like that. She deserves to be given flowers and expensive gifts, things that I could never afford to give her. No matter how hard I work, I could never afford something nice that she deserves. I am too much of a loser to be able to get the girl of my dreams something she deserves. I slam my locker door closed, not wanting to look at that single flower again before I head down the hall to get to my first class.

I could never give her nice gifts, I can't be good looking, I'm not athletic, I have nothing to offer her. When I look at these obvious facts, I know deep down in my heart, that I could never be with her. I am not worthy of her love.

As I turn a corner, I am greeted to the sight of a familiar person, that girl Lexi that Colomba was trying to cheer up the other day. Hanging from one of her arms is a basket that is filled with flowers, I look a little harder and I can tell that they are carnations. Colomba told me what they are once, she likes to plant them in her garden at home since she says that they have a beautiful scent. As I watch her, I see that she is handing out flowers to everyone who passes her. Whenever someone takes a flower from her, she tells them "Happy Valentine's Day!" with a cheerful grin. Only a few people seem grateful for her sweet gift, most chuckle behind her back as soon as they grab the flower. They chuckle about how "stupid" she is for wasting her money and time doing this since nobody would ever want to be her Valentine, so she is stuck trying to make people like her by doing something desperate like this. When I look at what she is doing, I don't see it as her trying to get some attention. It looks more like she's just trying to make people happy, but nobody seems to care about that, they just want to tease her. Lexi must be hearing what they are whispering behind her back since I see tears forming in her eyes which she tries to hide behind a cheerful smile as she continues to hand out flowers, telling people to have a good holiday. She is trying her best to be kind, but nobody cares, they are doing their best to make her feel miserable.

As I look at Lexi's miserable eyes, I remember what she said yesterday, how she wished that everyone would just love each other no matter what they looked like. My heart feels pity for her for only a moment before a sudden idea comes into my mind. I think of that single flower in my locker and the wonderful girl it is meant for. The pity in my heart fades as I feel hope rise in me and a dark smile crosses my face.

People start heading to their class before the warning bell rings, all except Lexi and I. She continues standing in the hall, her head hanging in misery as she gives up trying to give people flowers, and I head to the nearest bathroom. I enter it and only have to wait a moment before it is empty so that I can lock the door and I can complete the plan that I had just created in the hall.

Placing my hand over the Crow Medal, Shadow appears instantly on top of one of the stalls, she fluffs out her feathers before looking down at me.

"Good morning Master, happy Valentine's Day. What can I do for you on this lovely holiday?" I smile up at her, excited to get my plan started.

"Hey Shadow, I need you to transform me into the Crow, I have an idea." Shadow looks at me with curiosity, but doesn't say anything as she flies around me faster and faster until I blink my eyes and look in the mirror, seeing myself as the Crow. My smile grows wider at the sight. Closing my eyes, I whisper to the empty room, "Shadow, find Lexi." Shadow flies out of the bathroom as a shadow on the ground as she flies straight toward

Lexi who is wandering down the hallway alone. Shadow plunges straight into her heart and I speak to her, eager to tell her my plan.

Hello Lexi. She jumps in surprise and a few of her flowers drop from the basket.

"Who's there?" She looks around herself in terror, her fear getting worse when she realizes that there is nobody nearby.

I am the Crow. I am here to help you. She stops looking around herself, knowing that she will never find me. Her heart is still pounding, but her voice is calmer when she speaks again.

"How?" I smile when I realize that I have her.

People tease you for not looking the way they want you to, but even though they do that you still try to bring joy to others. You like this holiday because it reminds people to care about each other. Some people don't listen to this though, they continue to hate. Maybe you should make them listen, make them see how wrong they really are. I can help you with that, I can help you make them see how much love and acceptance can change the world. She stops for a moment to think about what I said before she asks the obvious question.

"What kind of power can you give me to help me do that?" I chuckle and I can feel her shudder a little as that chuckle echoes through her mind.

I can give you the power to make people love whoever you want them to. I can help you show all these people how to really care about each other no matter what they look like. She smiles wide, hope rising in her.

"Yes! Yes, I will do whatever you say!" I chuckle again, but this time she isn't afraid.

Good, I just need you to do something for me as soon as you get your powers. The fear returns in her a little bit at my words.

"What exactly do you need me to do?" Her voice is timid, so I try to reassure her.

It is alright. What I am asking you to do is something you will enjoy doing. I feel her slightly relax in her mind. I just have a specific person that I want you to get first. My lips pull up into a smile as I tell my eager new soldier what to do.

Chapter Nine
Colomba-
More Gifts

I am still rubbing my eyes as I enter my first class. Those roses really bothered my allergies, my nose is still running a bit. I bet my eyes are still a bit red too, I must look like a real mess right now. Class hasn't started yet, so everyone is just hanging out and chatting. I walk over to my seat, but stop when I see that there are already a few things on my desk in the front row. Moving closer, I can see what the objects are more clearly, candy and more flowers. Heart shaped boxes of chocolates and another bouquet of red roses lie on my desk. I release a small groan of annoyance at the sight of the roses. I don't know who left those, but I know I hate them, my eyes are watering again already.

Sitting down at my desk, I take the card off the ribbon wrapped around the stems of the roses before placing the roses under my desk. Hopefully that will keep them far enough away that they won't bother me. I open the card to see that they are from one of the guys in my class asking me to be his Valentine. I glance back at him to see him look away, he had obviously been watching me, seeing how I would react to his gift, but didn't want to be caught staring. When I look around the classroom, I notice a few of the guys look away from me nervously, obviously they had also been staring at me to see my reaction. Three boxes of chocolates with cards on top still lay on my desk, but I don't have time to examine them before the teacher starts class. Quickly, I place the chocolate boxes in my bag and pull out my notebook to start taking notes.

As my pencil flies across the paper, I'm writing down as much as I can as the teacher speaks a mile a minute. I feel stares drilling me in the back of the head. I know that some of those stares are probably from the guys who left those gifts, trying to figure out what's going on in my mind, trying to figure out if I have feelings for them too. Those stares make me uncomfortable because I know that I don't care for any of them like that and I know that I will have to break their hearts when I tell them the truth.

There are other stares that I feel though, and they aren't as friendly. I can feel the eyes of other girls on me and the gifts that can be seen in my bag. I glance at the girl sitting beside me and I can feel her jealousy as she looks from me to the gifts. She is jealous that I got so many gifts from guys while she didn't get anything. She wants the attention from the guys on this special day where you hope to have someone love you. I want to tell her that I didn't want any of this, I want to just have some peace but I keep getting bothered by boys today. I know what she would say though about my complaints though, she would say that I'm being stupid and that any girl should want this.

Why does everyone think that I should be happy with all this attention? The boys look at me and expect me to just melt over the gifts they have given me while the girls look at me like I'm an ungrateful idiot since I don't seem happy about the gifts. I don't want gifts, I want love, and I don't think that the boys who gave me these gifts really love me, and I don't love them. I always thought Valentine's Day was supposed to be this beautiful day where you celebrate the person you love, to everyone else though it seems to be just a day where you are supposed to give or take gifts. What happened to the love? What happened to the joy of the holiday? As I look down at the gifts in my bag, I think about how it is probably gone and never coming back, at least not any time soon.

When the bell rings at the end of class, I pick up my bag and rush out before any of the boys who gave me gifts can try to talk to me. Weaving through the crowd, I make it to my locker without anyone else bothering me. My fingers fiddle with the lock on my locker as my mind flashes through sad thoughts. I don't feel like breaking anyone's heart today. Hopefully they will take the hint with me running out like that and realize I'm not interested in them. I can hope, but with my luck I'm sure that one or two won't take the hint and I will have to tell them to their face that I'm not interested and I will have to break their hearts then. I rest my head against the cool metal of the locker, feeling completely defeated. Why must I constantly be chased by men I do not want? As I think this, my thoughts immediately go to Alex and the flowers he gave me this morning. Why can't they all just leave me alone?

I sigh softly as I lift my head off the locker and finish putting in the locker's combination. The door swings open easily, I open my bag to place the gifts on a shelf. I pause to look at them, wanting to feel joy in knowing that someone was kind enough to give me something like this, but I'm only feeling sadness. I look away from them, knowing that it is only going to make me feel worse to look at it another second. Pushing the thought of those gifts out of my mind, I start grabbing my books for my next class, hoping that the rest of the day will be peaceful. I realize that hope is pointless though since all that happened in just my first class, and I bet that I will have a lot more headaches as the day goes on.

Chapter Ten
Luis-
My Joy
Begins

I am back as my normal self, trying to make myself look like I don't know what is about to happen. I gave my newest soldier, my Flying Ace, her orders and then told her to wait until she saw myself and Colomba close together. To make her powers work, she needs to strike so that the first person or thing that the person she struck sees is who she wants them to be with. Whoever they see first will be the one they fall in love with, love at first sight in a way. For me it was love at first sight, for Colomba though it will be love at a millionth sight. This time, I will finally get the girl of my dreams, I will be with Colomba.

It is hard to not look excited. I can't let Flying Ace see my excitement since she might get suspicious, she might figure out that I am really the Crow. As the Crow, I told her that I wanted her to get Colomba first since I knew that a "guy named Luis" really cares about her and would treat her like a princess. Flying Ace was very excited about that idea, she said that she would be happy to do that since Colomba is very sweet and deserves to be with a guy who would treat her well and love her. I couldn't agree more. I try to look like a normal guy going through a normal day while trying to hold back the most excitement I've ever felt in my life. It doesn't take me long to find Colomba, I spot her at her locker putting some things away. As I get closer to her, I realize that she is putting away boxes of chocolates and some more flowers that she must have gotten in her last class. I feel a wave of jealousy come over me for only a moment, it quickly fades when I realize that in a minute or so she will never care about those gifts. All that will matter to her is having the two of us together. All the guys who have been giving her things will be very disappointed because from now on she will barely even look at them when I am around, they won't even have the slightest chance with her.

I walk over to Colomba as she pulls a book out of her locker. My heart pounds in excitement, knowing what is about to happen.

"Hey Colomba, how's it going?" I lean against the locker next to her, trying to look relaxed even though I am almost bursting as I wait impatiently. She smiles sweetly at me.

"I'm alright. How are you?" Over her shoulder I can see a small figure hidden in a doorway of a classroom. The figure is holding what looks like a bow and arrow.

"I'm doing great. What are you up to this Valentine's Day? Do you have your own

Valentine?" I say this in a teasing tone that makes her giggle.

"No, no I do not."

"How could you not have a Valentine? You're too sweet and…" I stop, feeling my stomach tying itself into knots, but when I see my newest soldier getting the arrow positioned on the bow, I feel my confidence grow. "And you're too beautiful." Colomba looks up at me with wide eyed shock, she isn't used to me complimenting her so openly. She looks at me like that for only a moment before the arrow flies through the air and hits her in the back before disappearing. Colomba lowers her head into her hand, her eyes closed as if she has a headache. She moans softly before she slowly lifts her head from her hand and smiles at me with more warmth than anyone has ever smiled at me with.

"Are you okay Colomba?" She is looking at me strangely, as if she is seeing me for the first time and she is captivated by me.

"Yeah. Do you really think I'm beautiful Luis?" I smile warmly at her, feeling that the question is ridiculous, anyone would believe that she is beautiful.

"Of course, anyone with eyes could see that." She lowers her head as she smiles, and her cheeks glow a bright red. She smiles as she looks back up at me. With a gentle hand, she reaches up and brushes my long bangs away from my eyes.

"You know, I've never said this to you, but you have beautiful eyes." My heart pounds in excitement. This is actually working!

"They're not as beautiful as yours."

Colomba giggles, so happy to hear my compliment. "Would you mind if I walked with you to class?" She beams at me.

"I would love that." Colomba walks closely beside me as we head down the hall, closer than she usually does.

"Would you like me to carry your books?" She looks at me as if I just offered her world peace on a silver platter.

"Yes please." She hands me her books that I hold in the hand farthest from her. As we walk our hands are so close together that they are almost touching. Taking a chance, knowing that I can't lose while she is under this spell, I hold her hand in mine. Her hand is so small in mine, my hand is practically covering hers. Colomba doesn't seem to mind though, she entangles her fingers in mine and smiles shyly up at me. I should have done this ages ago. I smile down at her with complete confidence, showing that I am happy holding her hand, her shyness quickly fades into pure joy.

I can feel some people staring at us with unhidden shock at seeing me holding Colomba's hand. These people who have always made fun of me, calling me a loser, probably never expected such a beautiful, wonderful girl like Colomba would ever be with me. A few guys look at Colomba and I with a different expression though, jealousy. I recognize a few of them as the ones who gave her gifts, I had seen their names on the cards attached to the gifts and such. They are jealous that I am with the girl they desire, I have won her, and they will never have her. Jealousy is usually the feeling I have towards others, it feels nice to be the one other people are jealous of. It is nice to finally have a life worth living. With Colomba, my life is something I can actually enjoy.

I walk with her to her next class, feeling as if I am walking on a cloud because I have reached Heaven.

Chapter Eleven
Colomba-
Pure Love,
Pure Hate

My second class is moving so slowly that I want to scream. I want to get back to Luis. We had to separate to get to our classes, but I wanted to stay with him. I only went in the class because I didn't want to get in trouble, and I don't want my absence to affect my grade. If I was even slightly less worried about those two things, I would have stayed with him. Everything seems so much darker in the world since I don't have him beside me right now. Why can't time move faster?!! I want to be with him so much!!

I have no idea what has come over me, I don't know why I suddenly feel so in love with Luis when just earlier today I only thought of him as a friend. What is up with that? How did this happen? Those questions quickly leave my mind though when I think about how happy he made me feel just by being close to me, how my heart leaped when he held my hand. As the previous questions leave my mind, a happier thought gets in my mind, how did I not see how amazing he is before today?

I have always known that he is a wonderful person. Luis is intelligent, sweet, fun to be around, artistic, and is always willing to do what he can to make me smile. He cares about me so much. Even when we were just friends he was always around when I needed someone and would always try to make me happy. When I think about all the things he has done to make me happy, I stop to wonder how long he has truly loved me. I just realized how much I cared about him today, but he has acted like this ever since I met him, so has he loved me this entire time? I think about this, but my thoughts are interrupted by the bell signaling the end of class. I practically jump out of my seat, eager to see Luis again, all the questions I had been thinking about completely forgotten.

As I step out of the classroom, I see two familiar faces waiting for me. One of them brings a smile to my face. I walk up straight to Luis and give him a big hug that Luis happily returns while the other person, Alex, looks at us with shock. He quickly tries to hide that shock with his usual confident grin.

"Hey, don't I get a hug too?" He asks this in a teasing tone, but I can tell that he is a bit hurt by this.

"Sorry no, just for him." I smile up at Luis, feeling content with the world now that I am in his arms. "Are you escorting me to class today?" Luis smiles at me so warmly that it feels like I'm going to melt.

"Of course." I hold his hand in mine.

"Good, I'm glad I have such a handsome gentleman to take me around." He chuckles as we walk down the hall together, with him gently holding my hand.

"Wait a minute!" Alex shouts out from behind us before running up to Luis and I to block our way. "There's no way that you two are dating, this has to be a joke." He is smiling at the two of us as if he is part of the joke, but his eyes show his distress. He cannot believe what is happening, and it scares him.

"Yeah, we are." Luis almost growls this at Alex, it is almost like Luis is challenging him. "Do you have a problem with that?" Alex doesn't respond, he just stares at Luis as if Luis is suddenly transforming into a werewolf right in front of him. Wow, it's a little strange seeing Luis stand up for himself. It's a good kind of strange though. I feel so proud of him.

Alex opens his mouth, but nothing comes out. In his eyes I see something frightening. The shock still stays there, but it is slowly fading to be replaced by pure hatred. His hate is directed right at Luis, but unlike me, Luis is not afraid. Luis smiles at this before the two of us walk right past Alex. A weird look comes over Luis' face for a moment, as if he is concentrating hard on something. His face returns to normal, but I don't pay attention, I'm too busy looking back at Alex.

"I can't believe that I've never noticed you before." Alex is looking right at a trashcan, but he is looking at it as if it is the most amazing thing he has ever seen. He kneels down beside it, eyes wide in wonder. "You are so beautiful." I burst out laughing as Alex straight up kisses the trashcan.

"Oh my gosh, did you see that?!" I ask Luis as the entire hallway laughs at Alex as he continues to kiss the trashcan like a complete weirdo. Luis chuckles as he looks back at Alex.

"I always knew that Alex was stupid, but I never thought he was that stupid though." Luis and I continue to walk while Alex continues to kiss the trashcan like a crazy person.

As I turn around to watch where I am going, the smile fades on my face for a moment as a thought hits me. Something isn't right here. What on earth made Alex do something like that? He was being all jealous of Luis and I only seconds before and then acts like he is in love with a trashcan. He even kissed the thing as if he thought it was the most perfect thing in the world. I look around the hallway, and I notice a few other strange things. I see several couples holding hands and giving each other lovey-dovey stares, but I know a lot of these people and I would never have expected them to be with the person they are with now. Some are holding hands with people they have openly stated that they hated, and some are with people that I have heard them making fun of before.

As Luis and I pass through the halls, I hold his hand, never wanting to let go. He is smiling down at me as he talks, his eyes full of love. He has been telling me about some weird customers that have come into his uncle's shop. Right now, he's telling me about a lady who came into the shop holding a rabbit, but she kept insisting that it was a dog. When he is telling me about how the lady screamed at another customer when they tried to tell her that it was a rabbit, a cold laugh interrupts him. The two of us look ahead to see Angela laughing as she looks at us holding hands.

"I can't believe it!" She stops for a moment to laugh again before she continues. "I didn't think that even a loser like you Colomba would ever sink so low as to date that freak!" She points a perfectly manicured finger at Luis and his happy face instantly turns into a glare of fury. "I thought that even you would have better taste than that!" I feel my face grow warm and I know that I am turning red. I'm holding back so much anger that I feel like I'm going to explode. I want to scream at her for being so mean to the man I love, but I am stopped. Luis rests his hand on my shoulder and gives me a comforting smile before he steps forward to stand in front of Angela. Angela looks a bit surprised and a little intimidated that Luis is standing in front of her like this. I can understand why she looks a little scared too, Luis just looks so confident and strong, not like he usually is.

"Angela, you should never make fun of people who are in love." Luis' voice is different, it is calm and quiet even though Angela had just been making fun of him. Somehow this voice he is using makes him seem scarier than if he yelled at her. Angela seems to think the same way since she is practically shivering in fear. "You wouldn't think it's so funny to make fun of people who are in love if you loved someone, and everyone laughed at you because of it. So don't be a stupid child and just leave us alone." Angela seems to gain back some of her courage since she smirks at him in her usual snobby way.

"Well I'm never going to have that problem 'cus I'm never going to fall for a loser like you." Angela walks away and around a corner with her nose in the air, like she owns the world, while Luis turns back to me, smiling warmly. The smile on his face makes him look so proud of himself, and I have to say that I'm proud of him too. I have never seen Luis stand up to people like that before, especially not people like Alex and Angela. He was so strong when he is usually so timid.

"Sorry about that." Luis says to me, but I just shake my head at him.

"Don't be sorry, I'm glad you did that, she needed to hear it." Luis holds me in a gentle embrace.

"Thanks, I just couldn't stand hearing her be mean to you like that." I nuzzle my head against his chest as he holds me tighter. It feels so nice to hear him say that he wanted to defend me. Alex has said that he would protect me before like when one of the Crow's transformed people was attacking the school, but that just made me feel mad and uncomfortable. When Luis says it though, it just feels so right.

Luis and I start walking down the hallway again, walking in a peaceful silence as we are both lost in our thoughts. A strange thought occurs to me that makes the smile leave my face. Why does it feel different when Luis says that he will protect me? It has always annoyed me when someone has done that before. Even when people I was friends with did it, I would hate it. If it was like that for everyone else before, why is this different? I know that I care for him in a different way than I have ever felt for anyone else, but I never expected that I would ever feel good about someone wanting to protect me like some damsel in distress, but it made me happy when Luis said it. Why is this so different? My mind tries to ponder over this when I see something that makes my mind completely freeze in my shock.

Angela is back, but she is now walking down the hall on the arm of a boy I never thought I would ever see her touch, let alone be with. She always thought of herself as a little princess and would never stoop to someone she thought of as ordinary, she thinks that she deserves a Prince Charming. In her eyes though the guy she is cuddling up to is less than ordinary if I am to believe things I have heard her say about him before. His name is Joel, the head of the Crow's fan club. He is one of the people in school that pretty much everyone makes fun of and treats like dirt. He is a small, scrawny guy who has interests in things that others view as weird. In the eyes of others, he is the perfect target to pick on. In Angela's eyes though, he is the last person on earth that she would ever think about being with. With that in mind, why on earth is she with this guy?!!!!

As I wonder this, the two pass us, saying

sweet things to each other about how much they are in love, and I hear Luis chuckle at my side. I look up to see Luis looking at Joel and Angela with a very proud look in his eyes and an almost scary looking smirk on his face. I stare at him, wondering how my sweet Luis could look so dark and almost… evil. Luis must have felt my gaze since he quickly lets the evil look in his eyes fade as he stares down at me with a loving gaze. His smile warms me to my core and the two of us keep walking down the hall.

Glancing back, I give one final look to Angela and Joel as they sit down on a bench and Angela cuddles up to him as if she is deeply in love. One of the biggest bullies in school is cuddling with the leader of the fan club for the Crow, the one who says that he will make the bullies suffer… Wait… the Crow?

I think of all the weird stuff that has been happening the past hour or so with everyone suddenly falling in love with someone they usually would never be with, and Alex falling in love with a trash can. When I think of these things, I can't help but wonder, is the Crow involved somehow? Has the Crow done something to make everyone act so weird? I think about how my feelings have changed so suddenly today, did the Crow do something to me too? My heart starts to race a little in fear, Luis must have noticed the sudden change of emotion in me since I feel him gently squeeze my hand. I glance up to see him smiling down at me, his sweet brown eyes look at me with pure love and all those negative thoughts are erased in my mind.

"How are you feeling Colomba?" His deep, gentle voice asks me with a little concern in his tone. I smile back at him, trying to reassure him.

"I feel wonderful, everything feels perfect when I am with you." Luis lets go of my hand so that he can wrap his arm around my shoulders and I rest my head against his chest, loving the feeling of being close to him. All my dark thoughts from only moments ago are completely gone, I don't think I could ever think of bad thoughts when I am with Luis. He really does make everything perfect. The two of us walk out one of the hall doors into the courtyard to enjoy the perfect day together. Then again, every day is perfect with Luis by my side.

Chapter Twelve
Luis-
Together
In the
Courtyard

Everything is so perfect right now. My Flying Ace has transformed the entire school. I think she has shot everyone with her arrows by now. The teachers aren't even teaching class, everyone is too much in love to think about going to class, let alone teach it.

Everyone is in love, including Colomba and me. Right now, we are sitting on a bench in the courtyard without anyone around to disturb us. All the flowers that Rosie, the girl I transformed into the Black Iris last year, planted are in full bloom. With all the flowers, the courtyard smells almost as good as the perfume Colomba is wearing. She is curled up against me on the bench, her head resting on my chest while my arm is wrapped around her. We have been sitting like this for a little over an hour just chatting. I was talking to her about my art projects I have been working on, and now she's telling me about some of the quilts that she and her grandmother have made recently. Everything feels so peaceful that it almost feels like I am in another world. I never knew that I could ever feel this happy.

When she finishes describing a quilt that they made last week with a seahorse on it, the two of us stop talking and just watch the birds flying from one tree to the next in the courtyard. There's something I really want to ask her now since everything feels so good, I want to see if it can be better. I haven't brought this subject up in a while with her and I want to see if she has changed her mind about it. If her mind has changed then everything really is perfect. If not, then I will still be happy because I finally have her as my own.

"Hey Colomba." She lifts her head slightly from my chest to look me in the face. Her eyes shine with curiosity, she could probably feel the seriousness in my voice.

"Yes Luis?" I'm afraid to ruin this beautiful moment, but I just have to know. I need to know what she really thinks.

"Colomba, what do you think about the Crow and what he's doing? Be honest with me please." She rests her head on my chest again and looks over at the flowerbed in front of us, a thoughtful expression has come over her face.

"You know, I've been thinking about that a lot recently. For a while I thought he was a monster transforming all these people, but things just feel different now. Every time Silver Dove stops one of the bullied kids that the Crow has transformed, everyone just goes right back to hurting each other as if nothing happened. You were always saying that the Crow is doing the right thing by doing these things since it will teach people a lesson. It would teach them not to be so cruel to each other, and you said that Silver Dove is getting in the way of the Crow teaching those lessons." She smiles softly as she looks back up at me. "You know Luis, maybe you were right about the Crow. I mean, everyone here is always trying to hurt each other no matter how many times Silver Dove stops whoever the Crow has transformed. Maybe Silver Dove should just let the Crow finish the job one day. Maybe then people will finally wake up and learn how to treat each other with respect. Maybe then everyone will finally be happy." I hold her closer so that she won't see the tears of joy forming in my eyes. It has finally happened, I have won, I have completely won. Alex is in love with a trashcan, Angela is in love with someone she absolutely hates in real life and makes fun of all the time, and I have the love of the most perfect girl in the world. Not only that, but she now approves of me as the Crow, she now accepts every part of me. Maybe now I can finally reveal who I really am once we get a bit more serious as a couple. We only just started dating today, I think we should take things slow considering she just started approving of the Crow today.

With Colomba by my side, I know that there is nothing I can't do anymore. With her support I will do things that I have only dreamed of doing. Knowing that she supports what I am doing will give me the strength to go even further as the Crow. I will give powers to more bullied kids like me and they will finally get rid of Silver Dove for me. I will unmask her and find out who she really is. After that, I will convince her to join my side so that we can fight side by side like we were always meant to be. The world will tremble at our power, but we will only harm the wicked, all the good people of the world will be safe. Once the people of this school have learned their lesson, I will rule over this school with Colomba at my side. I will be the most respected and feared ruler of all time, the people who have ever hurt me will regret everything that they have done to me. When I look down at Colomba in my arms, I think about how when I take over the school I can finally get her all the things she deserves. With the power I will have over this school, I will be able to give her all the nice things a sweet, beautiful girl like her should have. I can make all the old bullies buy her amazing clothes, jewelry, flowers, and anything else she likes as their punishment for their past crimes. She will never want for anything, everything will be given to her so that she will never have to struggle again. I will also make sure that her family is taken care of too. They will never have to work another day in their lives if they want. The good people will be rewarded in my new world while the evil will be punished severely. That's the way it should be. That is real justice. Sadly, justice isn't really seen in the real world, at least not until I run this world.

As I hold Colomba in my arms, Flying Ace

continues to ask for instructions as she flies through the hallways. Nobody has really noticed her, she stays in the shadows and most of the school is under her spell anyway and are too distracted by their love. If someone who hasn't been shot notices her, then she would just shoot them with one of her arrows so that they fall in love with someone and then they would just forget about her. They are too distracted by whoever they have fallen in love with to care. Flying Ace could just walk down the halls now and nobody would notice, she has shot her arrows at practically everyone now and the positive vibes are all over the place, everyone is feeling the love.

I hold Colomba close to me, but something feels… off. Suddenly something just doesn't feel right. This is wrong. I should be happier than I've ever been since I finally have the girl I've always wanted, but right now it just doesn't feel right. It just feels so… not real.

Pulling her in closer, I try to feel the same joy I had moments ago, but it is gone. It is gone and I don't think I'm going to get it back. I have what I want, what I've wanted for years, but now it doesn't feel like I'm actually living my dream. I am living in a fantasy that I can't truly enjoy. It is all fake.

Chapter Thirteen
Colomba-
Life is
Perfect

My heart seems to race as I feel Luis' hand in mine tighten its grip. I look up at his face to see the most perfect man in the world. As I look into his deep brown eyes, I can't help but wonder how I never realized how perfect her was before today. What was wrong with me? How could I be so blind to how sweet of a guy he is? He is absolutely perfect in every way.

We are walking down the hall and he looks so proud to be holding my hand as we walk together. It's almost as if he thinks that he's the lucky one, that's funny. I am the lucky one here. I am so lucky that a wonderful guy like him chose me, and no other girl snatched him up when I was too blind to see how amazing he is.

The two of us pass by Alex, he is still sitting beside the trashcan, saying sweet words to it as if he loves it while giving it little kisses. Angela is a little ways down the hall, cuddling up to Joel, a nerd that she would have never touched in a million years if you asked her yesterday. My thoughts wander away from Luis for a moment as I think about how strange this is. Everyone around me is acting completely weird. Why does Alex suddenly have a thing for that trashcan and why does Angela love a guy she thought was a complete dork just yesterday? Alex was flirting with me right before he started acting weird with that trashcan… weird, he seemed to change so suddenly, as if somebody made him do it, as if he was being controlled. Alex has been chasing after me ever since we got into high school, he wouldn't just give up all of a sudden like that, he's too stubborn to do that. Plus, I don't think he would have accepted losing me to Luis since he and Luis seem to hate each other for some reason. Having someone who he thought of as a loser (even though I can't see how he could ever think of anyone as spectacular as Luis could be a loser) get me instead of him would be far too much for him to take. He would have probably tried to do something mean to Luis, but instead he falls in love with a trashcan?

This does not make sense at all!! I thought about this earlier, but I didn't even really give it any thought or do anything about it even though I knew something was wrong!! What is wrong with me?!! All this weirdness may have something to do with the Crow!! Why didn't I do something to help?!! I'm usually always trying to help whenever something isn't right, but I let myself get distracted today!! How could I do such a thing?!! How could I do this to the school that I had promised that I would protect?!!

I lower my head in shame as a tear threatens to fall down my face. I'm Silver Dove, I'm supposed to protect the people of this school, not just let the bad stuff happen. When the tear is about to drip from my eye, I notice some strange movement from the corner of my eye. Glancing up, I look out the window to the courtyard to see what looks like a large creature with very large, white wings. Much too large to be anything ordinary, not anything around this area at least. I look hard out the window, hoping that I will catch another glimpse of that thing and figure out what it is.

"Is everything okay Colomba?" I look back at Luis, I had almost forgotten he was here in my worry. Why was I worrying though? I have Luis with me, nothing could ever be wrong when he is beside me.

"Nothing, I just thought I saw something. It's not important, you are what's important to me. Now what were we talking about again?" I smile up at him, and he gives me a gentle smile back that makes all of my thoughts disappear, all that matters is him right now. He starts to tell me about some of his plans for his future in the art world when he gets older while I listen excitedly about his dreams. As he excitedly talks about it, I wonder about what I was worried about a moment ago. What was I so concerned about? Everything is perfect, nothing could possibly be wrong right now. Everything is exactly as it should be.

Chapter Fourteen
Luis-
Something is
Wrong

The morning has passed by, this beautiful, beautiful morning, and Colomba is standing beside me as we wait for my food in the cafeteria. Colomba brought her own lunch, but she is willing to wait with me in line just so she can spend more time with me. She holds my hand gently, her perfect eyes looking straight into mine with adoration as we talk. I can't believe how lucky I am at the moment, but even though I am holding hands with the most perfect creature on the face of the planet, I somehow don't feel completely happy.

I pick up my tray from the lunch lady and Colomba and I head to our usual table. Nat is already sitting there, holding hands and making googly eyes at a guy I recognize from my math class. His name is Greg, a nice, but very loud and confident guy. Not the kind of guy I would have expected shy Nat to fall for. I can easily see my Flying Ace's influence here.

"Hey guys, how is it going?! How's your

Valentine's Day going?!" Greg says with his usual confident grin, much more loudly than he needed to since we are only a few feet away. Nat smiles at us, looking so happy when she sees Colomba and I holding hands.

"Finally! I knew that you guys would get together one of these days! When did this happen?" I smile at Colomba, and she smiles back proudly.

"It just happened earlier today, I just looked at him and realized just how much I have been missing out on for so long and knew that I had to take a chance to try and be with him. Thankfully, he loves me just as much as I love him." My heart seems to stop for a moment as I hear her say that she loves me. I am so joyful for only a moment before the feeling of not being complete comes back again. Now her lovely smile just seems like a cruel prank. Nat does not notice my sudden pain though, she is smiling as if everything in the world is perfect.

"Well I'm so proud of you guys, I know that you will be so happy together." Colomba giggles in joy while I clear my throat to ask a question that I feel awkward about saying.

"Thanks, you mind if we take off though, I think we would both like some privacy today?" Nat gives me a little knowing smile and a wink.

"Of course not, you too have fun." I lead Colomba to an empty table nearby, and she follows me as willingly as a little puppy. The two of us sit down together and Colomba moves closer, obviously wanting to be as close as possible to me. I clear my throat again, suddenly feeling nervous at having her so close.

"I'm so glad that you decided to hang out with me for lunch." She smiles at me as if I am the most precious thing in her life.

"Of course I would, I love you." My heart stops beating for a moment again when I hear those last three words. I have been wanting to hear her say that for almost two years now. I should feel happier than I have ever been before, but right now I only feel heartbroken.

"I love you too Colomba. I've loved you for so long, longer than you know." I look away from her loving eyes as one thought passes through my head. I just wish that I could believe this is real.

I look back down at Colomba to see that she is smiling at me with pure happiness. I wrap my arms around her in a tight hug and she rests her head against my chest. I should be enjoying this, but I know that she wouldn't be acting this way if she wasn't under the Flying Ace's spell. Without that she wouldn't have said that she loves me. Why would someone like her love someone like me?

I hold her tighter, trying to get those thoughts out of my mind. This is what I have always wanted, I should enjoy it. Colomba is in my arms, this is what I want. I have what I want, it doesn't matter how I got here, it just matters that I'm here. I keep repeating that in my head, but as I hold her, I can't help but feel guilty. I blink rapidly to try and get rid of the tears in my eyes. Colomba gently releases herself from my embrace so that she can look in my face, concern immediately clouds over her eyes.

"What's wrong Luis? Are you okay? You look so sad." Her perfect aquamarine eyes look into mine, absolutely terrified that something is wrong with me. I smile at her, trying to hide the pain I felt only moments ago.

"It's okay Colomba, it's just…" I take a moment to swallow my pride before I tell her the truth. "It just doesn't really feel real. It feels like I'm going to wake up any second now and this is going to be a dream, this feels fake. I feel like I am living in a daydream and you are just in my imagination. I have wanted to be with you for so long, it doesn't feel like I have finally achieved my dream of being with you. I haven't earned it." Colomba surprises me by smiling.

"You're crazy if you think that you need to do something to "earn me". I am not a trophy, I am the girl that loves you because you are you. You are a wonderfully sweet guy, you have always been so kind and such a good friend to me. You are smart and can talk to me about practically anything when most people our age wouldn't get it. You are always willing to help me and want to see me smile. That is why I am with you, because you are the person I want to be with. I love you Luis." Colomba's smile slowly fades as she leans in closer to me and closes her eyes. My eyes grow wide when I realize that she is trying to kiss me. Oh my gosh, this is it, this is going to be my first kiss and it's going to be with the girl of my dreams! I can't believe this, this is amazing! I can't believe that my biggest dream is coming true! As she gets closer to me though, I feel my heart shattering in my chest. This isn't right.

This isn't really what Colomba wants, this is just a spell that she is under.

I back away from her and she opens her eyes, pain clearly being shown in her gaze.

"What's wrong Luis? Do you not want to kiss me? Did I do something wrong?" I look away from her, seeing her in pain just makes what I am feeling even worse.

"It's not that at all Colomba, I'm just… I'm not ready." That is definitely not the reason, I've been ready to kiss her since the moment I met her, but this isn't right. Colomba smiles softly, as if she is trying to hide pain and disappointment.

"Oh okay, I understand. I can wait until you are more comfortable." She rests her head on my chest, probably to hide the sad look on her face. I hold her closer to make sure that she can't look up and see the pain I am hiding on my face.

This isn't right. She is under a spell, she isn't really Colomba, she is fake. The girl I am holding is just a fantasy, she is not reality. The girl I am holding is what I have always wanted, but she is not what she is supposed to be. I know this, I can feel this, but I can't do anything about it. I know that I can just tell Flying Ace to end the spell on everyone and things will go back to normal, but I can't, I won't. This is what I've always wanted. I will get used to this feeling and then I will be happy. I just need to keep remembering how horrible it is to love her and not have her love me back. If I keep thinking about that then I will realize that this is better. Even if it is fake, having her love me in this fake life is better than just being friends with her in real life. Besides, what's so great about reality anyway. Fantasies are better than reality.

Chapter Fifteen
Colomba-
Calling
Nonna

For some reason, the teachers aren't holding class anymore today. Everyone is just roaming the halls with their Valentines and enjoying the beautiful day. I just left Luis for a moment so that I can go into the girl's restroom because I need to call Nonna. I have to tell her about everything that has been happening today. I need to tell her about how happy I have become. Whenever something important happens in my life, I have to tell Nonna. That's basically a rule I live by, she is my best friend and I want her to know what's going on in my life.

As soon as the door closes, I look around to make sure that I am alone before I pull out my cell phone and start calling Nonna. It only takes a few rings before she answers.

"Young lady, you better have a good reason for calling me in the middle of a school day." She says this in a teasing tone, and I smile at the sound of it.

"Oh I definitely have a good reason for calling you." She chuckles softly.

"Well tell me Tesoro, I am dying to hear it." As I look into the bathroom mirror, I can see that I am practically glowing with joy.

"Nonna, I just had to call you! Something amazing has happened! I'm in love!" I hear her laugh on the other end with joy.

"That's wonderful Tesoro! Did you meet someone today?" I giggle softly.

"No, it's the strangest thing, I've known him for what feels like forever. I guess that I just didn't realize how I felt about him until today. Isn't that weird?" Nonna chuckles at me again.

"Well don't keep me in suspense, who is this boy?"

"It's Luis." My grandmother stays silent for a moment, as if she is processing what I just said.

"Luis? The boy who came to the house to draw your picture for the fair before school started?" She sounds so confused, but also a little... worried. What is going on?

"Yes, that's him. He's so wonderful. I can't believe that I didn't realize how great he is sooner. I was so blind." She is silent again, as if she is trying to think about what to say.

"Tesoro, this morning you told me that you didn't care for anyone like that. You told me that you didn't have anyone you even slightly thought of that way. What made you change so suddenly?" I do remember saying that, but it seems so silly now.

Why would I have said something like that when I had a wonderful guy like Luis in front of me?

"Well I guess I was wrong." She pauses again.

"Tesoro, this feeling just came all of a sudden, right?" Well that's a strange question.

"Yes, I guess so."

"And have you noticed that a lot of the other people in school have been acting strangely? Have some of them been acting like they're in love with people they usually wouldn't be with?" Now it is my turn to pause. Where is she going with this? I think back on a few things that I've seen today before I answer her.

"Well I guess there have been a few strange things going on. I mean, I did see Alex kiss a trash can and say he's in love with it, and Angela is now going out with a guy she always teased because she thinks he's a loser since he leads the Crow's fan club." I stop for a moment, thinking that I am seeing where she is going with this, but not wanting to believe it. "But it's nothing, I think. Just a few people being weird. It's high school though, everyone is a little weird." I hear Nonna sigh softly on the other end of the phone.

"I don't think that's what's going on Tesoro, I think that this might be the work of the Crow." I feel my heart race in my chest at her words.

"What are you talking about?" My voice breaks as I ask her this and I can feel the tears threatening to fall down my face.

"I'm talking about the reason why

everyone is acting strangely and why you have suddenly fallen in love with someone you weren't interested in this morning. Maybe the Crow has given someone the power to make people fall in love or change peoples' emotions." I can't help but laugh at what she said.

"Oh c'mon Nonna, that's silly. Why would the Crow do something like that? It just seems so weird. It doesn't sound like his style at all. The Crow is all about causing mayhem and destruction, not making good things happen, like people falling in love." She lets out a groan of confusion.

"I don't know, maybe he did it so that Silver Dove would be distracted so that he could do something while you were busy being in love. Love is the most distracting thing in the world." I shake my head, not wanting to listen to what she is saying, not wanting to believe it.

"This can't be one of his tricks, this feels so real!" My voice sounds panicked, it feels as my entire world is crumbling in front of me.

"I know that Tesoro, but maybe you should just take a look around as Silver Dove just to make sure. Please, just do this for me. I am your grandmother, I want you to be happy and fall in love with someone one day, but I want it to be real love. Can you please do this for me?" I take in a deep breath to try and calm myself and keep the tears back before I speak.

"Alright, I'll do it for you. I don't want this to be fake though." I almost sound like I'm begging to her on the phone, praying that this isn't fake. "I'm sure that everything is alright."

"I hope so too Tesoro. Good luck." We both hang up and I take in a deep breath while I leave the bathroom. Leaning against the wall on the other side of the hall is Luis. My heart melts when I see him waiting for me patiently. I have to force the sweet thoughts out of my head as I walk up to him.

"Hey Luis, my grandma just reminded me about something I need to do. I'll find you after I'm done, okay?" Luis smiles eagerly at me.

"Oh, okay. Anything I can do to help?" I shake my head, trying not to look at him.

"No, thank you for asking though, it is very sweet." I make the mistake of looking into his face for a split second. In his eyes I see disappointment since I didn't want his help, as well as another emotion that I don't understand, confusion. What I don't understand though is why is he confused? What is confusing about what I just said?

I try to forget about this as I say good bye to him, give him a quick hug, and then walk down the hall to find a janitor's closet or something so that I can transform without fear of anybody finding me as Silver Dove. I don't think that will be a problem though.

Now that I am actually looking around, and not just looking at Luis, I notice some strange things. Some people are latched onto each other in happy couples, while some people are coupled with other people I wouldn't expect, people they never would have talked to before. Right now, I see the snobby head of the cheerleaders on the arm of Demetrius, the smartest guy in school, a guy that a lot of people make fun of since they view him as a complete loser. Sitting on a bench is a guy that I have heard is a part time model and is very vain, who has his arm wrapped around a girl that a lot of people make fun of since she is poor and has to wear old clothes that make her not look very good.

When I look at them, I finally start seeing the truth in what Nonna had said. All the people who are usually bullies are now being all lovey-dovey with people they used to pick on. They would have never acted like this unless they were under some sort of spell. As I think this, I see Angela and Joel sitting on the ground in the hall. Angela is resting her head on his shoulder as she tells him all about her hopes and dreams for the future. Most of these dreams involve marrying a rich guy and living the life of luxury for the rest of her life, I doubt she knows that Joel is far from rich since she is still claiming that she loves him. As I walk a little farther, I see Alex sitting next to the trashcan he fell in love with earlier today. He is currently giving endless compliments to the trashcan like he usually does with me, and he is also decorating the trashcan with flowers as he tells it how "beautiful" it is. It takes all of my self-control to not laugh at him. He is under a spell; I shouldn't tease him when he doesn't have control over himself.

It doesn't take me long after that to find a janitor's closet in an empty hallway. I slip inside so that I can place my hand over the Silver Dove Pin and say, "Peaceful warrior." The closet instantly fills with light, I close my eyes and open them again a moment later to see that I have transformed into

Silver Dove. Opening the door, I have to move carefully out the door so that my wings won't get stuck in the doorway. I move carefully in the hallway, my eyes scanning the hallway for anything suspicious. I turn the corner and I am surrounded by the couples again under the spell.

As I walk through the crowd, none of them even really look at me, they are too busy looking at the person they are in love with. Or should I say, the person the spell says they should love. When I look at them, I see people who have been bad mouthing me as Silver Dove locked under this spell. I think of all the mean things they have said to me, how much it hurt me. As I look at them now though, I see the obvious. Their words don't matter, right now they need me to break the spell on them so that they can return to their normal lives. They may not want me, but they need me. A hero's job isn't supposed to be liked, it is supposed to be about protecting people. A hero shouldn't care about what people think of them, it does not matter. I do not need them to love me, it doesn't matter if people support me or not. What matters is that I do what I think is right, and what is right is breaking this spell over everyone.

My eyes scan through the crowd, but all I see is loving couples. I make sure to move slowly so that I will not miss anything. With how calm everything has been today, I wouldn't be surprised if this search will last a while. Whoever the Crow has transformed knows how to hide, I just need to learn how to seek.

Chapter Sixteen
Luis-
My Flying
Ace

Colomba just left me a few moments ago, and I feel very confused. Why did she want to get away from me like that? With this spell over her, she would want to be around me all the time, just like how I always want to be with her. What was so important for her to do that it made her want to go against the spell? What on earth did her grandmother say to her that would make her want to be away from me?

Well, if she needs to get something done, I should probably do the same while I have a moment alone. I haven't really been checking up on my Flying Ace in a while, I should probably ask her about her progress. I walk into the restroom, quickly making sure that nobody is inside, before I place my hand on the Crow Medal so that Shadow appears on the bathroom counter. She is looking at me as if she is a parent who is really disappointed in their child.

"What have you done?" Her voice is calm,

but I can hear the rage boiling inside her from her tone. I look at her, knowing exactly what she is talking about, but not wanting to say it out loud.

"What?" I see her feathers ruffle slightly in fury.

"What did you do to Colomba? To everyone in this school?" I feel my hands clenching into fists at my side.

"I did what I knew that I should do. Lexi needed to become my next soldier considering what she was going through and I thought this power suited her. You haven't really complained about me transforming people in a while, so why are you mad now?" Shadow is practically a ball of fluffed out feathers now in her rage.

"You are smarter than this Luis, you know why I am upset with you. You didn't give her those powers because you thought it "suited her", you did it because you wanted Colomba to love you. Admit it, you know that you can't hide from me." I know that I can't hide from her how I feel, but I still don't want to say it.

"Just shut up Shadow! I don't want to hear this!" Shadow opens her wings wide and flies over to me, landing on my shoulder. From that spot she is now looking down into my eyes and I see her anger burning in her black eyes.

"You need to hear it, because the truth is something you need to understand. You need to understand before you make a mistake that you will never forgive yourself for." I turn my head away from her, not able to stand looking at her anymore. "You have wanted to be with Colomba since the day you met her, but now you are forcing her to be with you. You must know that this isn't right. You are a good young man and should know that you shouldn't play with the emotions of others, especially the ones you care about."

"Shadow-" my words are practically a whisper as I try to hold back tears. Shadow can probably see this, but she doesn't care, she keeps on scolding me.

"Colomba has always been so kind to you, she has been the greatest friend you have ever had. How could you betray her like this? How could you force her to love you? This is not how you make yourself happy, you can't force people to like you, no matter how much you may care for them!" I am breathing hard as I try to keep back my own rage, but that doesn't last when I hear her say that last part. When I hear that, I explode.

"Shut up Shadow! Transform me into the Crow! I don't have time for all this, I have work to do!" Shadow was actually so surprised by my harsh, loud words that she jumped off my shoulder and is flying in place near my head.

"But Master-"

"No buts! I am your master, don't you forget that, and I ordered you to transform me into the Crow now! I have work to do!" I can hear Shadow sigh softly before she begins to fly faster and faster around me in a black blur. I close my eyes for an instant, and as soon as they open again I am the Crow. I don't waste a moment; I immediately speak to my Flying Ace within her mind.

Flying Ace! She responds so quickly it

was almost like she knew I was going to call her.

Yes Sir! Her voice is loud, as if she is a soldier addressing a general. I guess, to her, she kind of is.

What is your progress so far?

I have shot practically everyone in the school. I thought it would be best to do it slowly to not arouse suspicion. After I am done here, I will start to move outside of the school and start taking over the town. I bet we can have complete control of Drew's Hollow by sundown. She sounds so proud of herself, and I have to admit that I'm kinda proud too, but I won't be telling her that any time soon. I think that the Flying Ace has gotten farther than any of the other people I have transformed before. Everyone else just scared everyone, but she is actually controlling them, she almost has the hearts and minds of everyone in this school under her control. This is absolutely perfect. I don't let my happiness show to her, instead I make my tone sound as if I am only a little pleased at how well she is doing.

Good, good. Have you seen any sign of Silver Dove? At the moment, she is the only one who can defeat the two of us, but I haven't seen anything of her at all today. Even though strange things are happening, she is nowhere to be found.

No Sir, all is quiet. She must have been one of the first I shot since she hasn't seemed to notice that things are different.

That must be it. I may not like Silver Dove, but I do recognize that she is pretty smart. She has found ways to defeat every one of my soldiers so far, but she hasn't figured out that something strange is going on here? She must be her normal self, under the spell of my Flying Ace.

Yes, it is strange, but I suppose we have one less threat to worry about. Keep up the good work, soon the entire world will be under our spell and the world will be a more peaceful place because of the two of us.

Flying Ace continues to scan the hallways. She doesn't even have to hide anymore, she is flying around in plain sight since practically everyone is under her spell and is too wrapped up looking romantically into the eyes of whoever she made them fall in love with. They are too in love to notice anything around them besides the person they adore. I look through her eyes as she looks at the couples. The couples are looking at each other with complete adoration, just like how Colomba was looking at me only a few minutes ago. A sudden pain stabs me in the heart at the thought.

No, I can't let myself think about that now. I currently have what I have wanted for so long, I have the love of the girl I adore, I can't let myself think about those stupid thoughts I was having earlier. I have what I want and that's what matters, right? I just need to keep reminding myself about that, I have what I truly want.

Chapter Seventeen
Colomba-
The Battle

I fly through the hallway, the tips of my wings brushing the walls on either side as my eyes scan the crowd beneath me. I may be here, but I wish I was standing beside Luis. I hate being away from him. Each second away from him feels like torture.

I don't understand why Nonna is wanting me to do this, can't she just accept that Luis and I are in love? Why can't she just let us be happy? I fly around a corner and look down at the couples beneath me who aren't even noticing me since they are too busy being in love. I'm so jealous of them right now. I just need to do a quick scan of the school and then I can get back to Luis, Nonna would be okay with that, I'm sure. I feel a little happier as I think that, but that happiness does not last long. I turn around another corner and see something that immediately stops me, and I instantly know that I won't get to see Luis again soon.

Around thirty feet in front of me is a girl

around my age, but she isn't walking around with everyone else. She is flying above them, like me, thanks to a beautiful set of snowy white wings. The winged girl is wearing what looks like an old Roman toga and a silver colored mask that completely covers her, only small slits are open so that she can see, but they are too small for her eyes to be seen. What catches my eye is that in her hands are a bow and arrow, as if she is about to go hunting. With all the Valentine's Day decorations and her outfit, it automatically makes me think that she looks like Cupid wearing a mask.

This strange figure turns their head, and they spot me. The two of us just watch each other, unsure of what to do, before she makes up her mind and flies down the hallway, trying to get away from me. All thoughts leave my mind, I take off after this strange person, wanting to see what all this is about.

She flies very quickly, and I have to push myself very hard to keep up with her. When things are looking her way, when it looks like she is moving a bit farther from me, she does something weird. From the corner of my eye, I see someone who is standing alone (not in a couple like everyone else), they are pointing up at the two of us flying above them and shouting at everyone to look. Nobody looks at us though, they are too busy looking deeply into the eyes of the person they are holding. The person with wings flying in front of me quickly looks down at this person and places an arrow on their bow, aiming it right at them. I put on an extra burst of speed, terrified that she is going to hurt them, but I am once again surprised. She fires the arrow at them, and it hits them square in the chest and disappears in a second. It almost looks like the arrow was absorbed into them. The person looks very confused for a moment before they look around and see a bird outside the window. They look at the bird as if they are looking at the most beautiful thing in the world.

"Where have you been all my life?! I don't know if you believe in love at first sight, but I definitely do now!" The bird is frightened by their loud voice and quickly flies away. The person looks so afraid seeing the bird fly away. They run out the door and chase after the bird as if their life depends on it. As soon as the weirdo with wings sees what happened, they continue flying away from me. I don't move for a moment, too upset to think about chasing them. Nonna was right. The Crow did cause this to happen. He gave someone the powers to make someone fall in love, it looks like, with the first thing they see. Is that what happened to me and Luis? I think back and realize that I only started feeling that way all of a sudden and for no reason at all. All of this, all of the amazing things I have felt today, they have all been a lie. I am not in love, it was all a fantasy. My heart feels as if it is crumbling in my chest. I just lost the most beautiful feeling I have ever felt in my life. It feels as if I have lost someone I love, in a way, I guess I have. Tears fall from my eyes and slip underneath my mask. The tears get caught there, trapping their heat beneath my mask, making my already warm face even hotter.

Looking ahead, I see the one who caused

all of this, the one who caused my heartbreak. That girl with wings is flying around a corner, moving as fast as they can to get away from me. My hands are curled so tightly into a fist that I can feel them shaking. How dare she make this happen? She will pay… no, she isn't the cause of this, the Crow is. He will have to learn his lesson, but I need to take out this threat first before she causes any more problems. I open my wings wider and take off as fast as I can after her. Trash and other papers scatter around the hallway as I fly faster than any other living thing. My body turns sideways so that I can turn around one corner. I do this so quickly that my wings almost hit the floor and ceiling before I turn myself back around.

It only takes me a moment to find that strange person again. She has her eyes locked on someone with their back turned away from her, someone who does not seem to be under her spell. She puts one of her arrows to her bow, aiming it straight at the unsuspecting person. I put on an extra burst of speed and open my arms wide. I ram straight into her waist with my shoulder, wrapping my arms around her as I tackle her, the two of us slamming into the lockers on the other side of the hall. The massive crash from us slamming into the lockers seems to fill the entire hall. The couples all scatter, trying to protect the one they love from the fight that is obviously about to happen.

Picking myself up off the floor, I shake out my wings spreading them out wide to try and look fierce to this new opponent.

"Who are you, and what are you doing to

the people in my school?" The girl with the mask stands up and spreads out her wings. I can easily see that they are actually a bit bigger than mine. Well… my plan backfired a little, now I look like an idiot, great. They look over at me, well at least I think they are, it's hard to tell with that mask covering every bit of their face.

"Does it matter?" I hate it when these villains answer a question with a question, it is super annoying and is a real jerk move. The masked girl just chuckles at my annoyed face. "You'll be under my spell soon anyway and you'll forget all about this. You will be too focused on who or whatever you fall in love with, and you will never give me another thought." She laughs again and I quickly realize that I need to figure out a way to defeat her as fast as possible before she shoots me with another one of her arrows. I can't let myself get distracted or she will cast her spell on everyone and there will be nobody who can stop her.

"Can you at least tell me why you are doing this with the power that the Crow has obviously given you? Why do you want to make everyone fall in love like this?" I notice her hand tighten around her bow in anger, I seem to have asked an irritating question to her.

"Because people need to learn." She starts walking toward me, holding that bow so tightly that it almost looks like she is going to snap it in half.

"Learn what?" I start backing away, trying to keep some distance between us, feeling a little nervous seeing how angry she is. She kinda looks a little crazy with how angry she is.

"They need to learn how to love each other no matter what they look like!!" I feel my eyes suddenly narrow in thought. 'love each other no matter what they look like', where have I heard that before? She loads her bow as quick as a flash and fires it directly at my face, I manage to move my sword in front of my face just in time. The arrow bounces off my sword with a loud clang only an inch from my nose. When the girl sees this, she lets out a growl of anger before she opens her wings to fly straight at me, raising her bow to hit me with. Leaping out of the way, I roll along my winged back right before her bow would have struck me across the head. She turns her body to face me, every part of her is stiff in her rage.

"They need to learn that they can't just be mean to somebody just because they are ugly!! They need to love everyone even if they look like a freak!!" Wait… I think I know who this is now. The one person who I have seen getting hurt recently because people keep telling her that she looks like a freak.

"Lexi?" Her arm swings forward, carrying the bow with it in a large arch heading straight into my gut. I move away in time, but not very far, I can still feel the bow brush against my armor making a loud scratching sound that sets my teeth on edge. Lexi doesn't waste a second, as soon as she realizes that she missed me she brings the bow over her head to strike down on my helmet. When I realize what she is doing, I lunge forward and tackle her. The two of us fall to the ground in a crumpled heap, the two of us squirming together, me trying to grab her to keep her down and her trying to get out of my grip. As my patience wears thin, I slap her across the face with my wing, stunning her for a moment. This gives me the time to grab both of her hands, pinning her to the ground.

"Listen Lexi, you've got to stop this!! The Crow doesn't really care about you, he is just using you!! Let go of these powers before you hurt anyone else!! Please Lexi!!"

"*Don't call me that!!!*" She pulls her legs beneath me and kicks me right in the chest. I fly backward and land on my back, my wing landing awkwardly underneath me. She picks herself up quickly, glaring down at me menacingly through her mask. "I am the Flying Ace now!! I'm not that pathetic kid anymore!! Don't you ever forget that!!" She brings her foot up high right above me, obviously trying to stomp her foot on my face. Rolling out of the way, I sweep my foot around just as she stomps her foot. My sweep catches the foot she stomped with, and she tumbles to the ground as I make contact with her. This time I am the one to pick myself up while she is on the ground.

"You were never weak Lexi, just hurt! You can't do this to everyone just because a few people said mean things about you. Things that are not true, by the way! You are not a freak just because you look different than what people say you should look like. You just look different, but that's what makes you human. There is nothing wrong with you." She scoffs at me as she gets up off the ground.

"As if!! I am a freak!! So I need to do this to make sure that nobody gets hurt like me again!!

If everyone in the world is in love, then nobody will hurt anybody ever again!! You don't know what it's like for me! You're probably beautiful under that mask! You don't know what it's like for everyone to think you're ugly." I don't back down, I move closer to her, staring right into her masked face.

"Maybe I don't know what it's like in your life, but I don't need to be hit by a meteor to know it hurts." She cocks her head to the side in confusion at my words. "Just because I don't live the same life as you, doesn't mean that I can't see that you are in pain!" The grip on her bow loosens and I can tell that she is actually listening to my words. I take a chance and make my tone less angry, using a more comforting voice, a gentle voice full of understanding.

"I do not think that that you are ugly. You were passing out flowers to everyone to make them happy this morning. I could never view someone who does that as ugly. The person you are acting like right now though, that is an ugly person." Apparently, that was a bad choice of words, she swings the bow at me again, striking me right across the face. When I stumble back, this gives her the opportunity to load another arrow into her bow. I look back just in time to see the arrow as it flies straight into my chest, right over my heart. I hold my hand over that spot as the arrow disappears while the Flying Ace laughs in her victory. My heart aches as one person passes through my mind, Luis. I think about his sweet smile, how he is always able to make me laugh even when it feels like my world is crashing around me, and I think about how wonderful it feels to have him hold me in his arms in a tight hug. As I think about all of this amazing things about him, one dark thought invades my mind. What I am feeling isn't real. The incredibly beautiful feeling of love that I have for him is just a lie that the Flying Ace has created within my heart.

Images and memories of Luis pass through my mind one after the other, making my head spin and my heart break in my chest. Tears race down my cheeks and I break down in sobs as the Flying Ace stares at me in complete confusion. She probably thought that as soon as she shot me, I would run off with someone, thinking I was in love with them and she could go on her merry way causing mayhem and destruction like she was earlier. Instead, she is stuck here awkwardly watching me cry like a baby while she tries to figure out what to do. More than anything right now, I want to go be with Luis. I am tired of battling this girl who is just making me feel worse about everything in my life.

"What is going on?" I'm not sure if she is asking herself or if she is talking to the Crow who is probably watching all of this go down through her eyes. If she is asking the Crow though, I don't think that he will have an answer for her. I think that he would be thinking the same thing the Flying Ace is thinking right now, that I am acting absolutely crazy. I'm not crazy though, I am heart broken. There is a difference, not a very big difference, but still a difference.

"You may think that making people fall in love would make everyone happy, but you have just made me miserable with it! You broke my heart when I realized that this was just a spell and that it was fake... No, you didn't just break my heart, you broke my entire existence! More and more people are going to wake up from this little dream and you will be hurting them too! You think that you are helping, but you are just hurting them! *Just like you have hurt me!"* My rage and pain boils over at those words and I swing my fist into her chest. In her surprise, she didn't have time to dodge, and I hit her dead on. She flies through the air around twenty feet down the hall before falling to the ground. The Flying Ace tries to stand up, only to fall back down due to her wobbly legs. I fly over to her, ready to hit her again, but she is ready for me this time.

She swings her body forward so that her wing swats me out of the air, sending me into a locker. I fall to the ground right in front of her. I get up into a kneeling position, breathing heavily as she does the same. The two of us are now face to face again as we kneel on the ground, too tired to get up. We glare at each other through our masks, rage being shared between us. As we glare at each other, I notice something behind her that immediately makes me forget about my pain and anger. Sitting on the floor down the hallway is Alex. He is sitting in front of his trashcan, kissing it and telling it how much he loves it. Alex is so focused on the "love of his life", that he doesn't seem to have noticed that there was just a battle going on only twenty feet away from him.

"Lexi, look over there. Look at what you have done." She is too confused by my suddenly calm tone to even get mad that I used her real name. She turns around to see Alex start to kiss his trashcan again. "You said that you wanted to make people be in love. To be in love is to be happy. Do you honestly think that he is happy right now? Can he be truly happy if he is forced to be in love with a trashcan? Can anyone be happy if they are forced to love anyone?" The Flying Ace looks back at me with confusion shown all over her face. It's obvious that she doesn't really know what to do, she doesn't know whether she needs to fight me again or to listen to what I have to say. The Flying Ace doesn't answer any of my questions, so I keep talking before she decides to try and hit me again.

"Love can't be fake if you want to be truly happy. It has to be one hundred percent. Just because you want the world to be different, doesn't mean you should make it different. People need to decide for themselves about how they should act and what they should feel. If they decide to be better people, that's great, if they want to be a jerk then that's their choice, and it is your choice as to whether or not they hurt you. You can just walk away and remember that their words are just that, words. They hurt at the moment, but you choose whether or not you believe what they say and let it stick with you." She lowers her head and I can faintly hear her crying beneath her mask.

"I just wanted everyone to love each other so that nobody will have to feel the pain I felt. I know I'm ugly-"

"You are not ugly Lexi." I tell her in a stern voice that kind of reminds me of my grandmother when I was little and I would get in trouble. "They told you some mean lies and because you heard them so often you started to believe it. Maybe the next time you start believing what some mean people say remind yourself of this, if they are mean people, should I really expect them to tell the truth?" She looks from me to Alex, then down to the ground. She responds to me in a soft whisper.

"But wouldn't this be better, having everyone in the world like each other? That way we would be happy?" I look at her as if I am a mother condemning her child for doing something wrong.

"I think you mean, so that way *you* would be happy." She quickly glances away from me, obviously feeling embarrassed. "Lexi, no matter how much you may want it, you can't make people like you." My heart shatters in my chest as I think about Luis. "You may love someone with all your heart, but that doesn't mean that they have to love you. Please, you have to realize that you can't do this. People should be able to choose who they love, not be forced to love someone." The Flying Ace stares at me, unsure of what to do while I hope that she will make the right decision. The two of us wait in an awkward silence while I know that there must be chaos inside her mind because the Crow is probably screaming orders at her right now. I can only wait for her to decide who she will listen to.

Chapter Eighteen
Luis-
My Decision

I don't know what to do, everything just seems so mixed up in my mind. Although I am still standing in the bathroom as the Crow, I feel as if I am miles away. I stand still, unsure about what to do while my soldier screams in my head, begging me to tell her what she should do. For the first time ever, I think about what Silver Dove is saying. I think about how Colomba has been acting today. She wouldn't be acting this way if she wasn't under a spell. All of that isn't real, and that's what I want, something that's real. For the first time ever, Silver Dove is right. I can't keep living a lie, my heart will just keep slowly breaking knowing that I am forcing Colomba to be with me.

Master! Crow! Please tell me what I need to do! Should I keep fighting her or not?! I don't know what needs to be done! What are your orders?! Her voice seems to echo in my brain. I lower my head, feeling guilty for what I have done to everyone, for what I have done to the one I love.

No Flying Ace, this needs to end, and it needs to end right now. We can't keep this up any longer, it's time for us to get back to reality. Shadow, it's time for you to come back.

Shadow leaves the Flying Ace, and a blinding light fills the hall for only a moment before Lexi has transformed back into her usual self. Shadow flies through the hall as a shadow on the wall while Silver Dove is talking to Lexi, making sure that she is alright. Shadow flies around the school, passing by people who are coming out of their spell. I watch as Angela and Joel quickly get out of each other's arms, looking at the other person as if they are a disgusting troll. Even in my misery I can't help but laugh at that. It doesn't take long before Shadow makes it back to me. She flies straight through the bathroom door and back into the medal as I turn back into myself.

Usually after I have done something as the Crow and Silver Dove has defeated me, I feel really angry. I don't feel like that today, today I feel guilty. What did I do? How could I do something like that to Colomba? I can't believe I'm saying this, but Silver Dove was right. I can't just force her to like me. I want to be with her, but not like that. If I want it to be real, then I need to work at it.

I look at myself in the mirror and ask

myself the question that I'm afraid to get the answer to. Even if I did work harder on it, would she ever date someone like me?

I look at myself in the mirror and I hate what I see. I see a scrawny kid with lank hair that hangs in his face. Dark, miserable eyes glare at me through the curtain of this kid's bangs. What I see is a pathetic kid who the world views as a mistake. I take a water bottle out of my backpack, open it, and splash the water at my reflection. The water streams down the mirror, making my reflection look messed up, but I can still see the miserable eyes glaring at me.

I turn away from the mirror, not wanting to see that image anymore. I grab my backpack off the counter and head out of the bathroom and into the hallway. Everyone is in the hall now, heading to their next classes and talking about Silver Dove and the Flying Ace. Some of the people that I know had been under the Flying Ace's spell look a bit dazed and confused, but they appear to be alright.

As I walk down the hall, a little bit of my gloom disappears when I see Colomba. She has the same confused expression as all the other people who have just been released from the spell. I walk up to her, happy but also uncomfortable at seeing her. I am always happy when I am with Colomba, but today I am also uncomfortable because I know what I have done to her, but she remains clueless.

"Hey Colomba." She turns around and smiles at me, but her smile seems to be a bit of an embarrassed one.

"Oh, hey Luis. How's it going?"

"Doing alright, are you okay? Did you have any problems with that person the Crow transformed, the Flying Ace or whatever she called herself?" She blushes so much that practically her entire face is scarlet in embarrassment.

"Yeah, I kinda did. Apparently, she had the power to make people fall in love with the first person they saw after she shot you with her arrows. I guess you were the first person I saw after she shot me." I look at her, I look at the most perfect girl in the world. I want to tell her that a spell didn't have to make me love her, but instead completely different words leave my lips.

"I guess you must have been the first person I saw too after she shot me. That was really weird, wasn't it?" Her embarrassment fades as she smiles up at me.

"Yeah, that was really weird. Out of all the powers the Crow has given people, this has to be the strangest." I nod at Colomba as she speaks, her embarrassment is gone, and a cheerful smile is lighting up her face. "I don't get this at all, I wonder why he wanted her to have that power. I mean, it wasn't really destructive like all the other ones have been. What was he hoping to accomplish from all of this?" I look down at her as we walk down the hall. He was trying to win you over, that's what he was trying to do. I think that in my mind, but my lips stay silent, I just keep walking and smiling with her, just trying to pretend that my heart isn't breaking.

"No idea, maybe he just wanted people to love each other." Colomba looks up at me, smiling as if I am being silly.

"Yeah right, as if the Crow would want to do anything like that. He doesn't strike me as the romantic type." I smile back down at her, I want to tell her that he is only romantic when it comes to you, but I keep my mouth shut. The two of us walk down the hall, talking about what had happened today with the Crow and the Flying Ace while I feel my heart aching even more with each passing second.

Colomba leaves me so she can go to her next class. I stand alone in a hallway full of people, but I feel more alone than I have ever been in my entire life. The whole world is crumbling around me as I walk to my next class. My world is ending and nobody can save me, nobody can save me because I caused this misery, I caused it and I deserve it. I am a monster.

Chapter Nineteen
Colomba-
Heartbreak

As I sit in class, my head resting on my head as I try to pay attention. As I glance around the room though, I don't think anybody else is paying attention anyway. Everyone seems to be off in their own little world in their minds, not even the teacher seems to be very into their teaching mode. I'm pretty sure that everyone is thinking about what happened with the Crow and the Flying Ace. If that's what they are daydreaming about, then I am definitely a part of the group. My mind is taking me through every minute of what happened when I was under the Flying Ace's spell. I remember the first moment when I started feeling as if I loved Luis, I remember wanting to stay with him every second, and I remember the heartbreak I felt when I realized that the beautiful emotions I was feeling were all a lie. Today has just been a major roller coaster for my heart, I almost want to just go to bed and sleep until tomorrow so that today can just be over with, I'm tired of today.

I feel that same pain in my heart when I think about Luis. What on earth am I going to say when I talk to him again? We spoke for only a minute after we got over the Flying Ace's spell, how are we going to move on after what happened? I mean we were professing our love for each other only an hour or so ago, how can two friends move on from that? This is going to be so awkward. I don't want it to be awkward with Luis and I though, he's one of my best friends and I don't want this to ruin our friendship. I wouldn't lose our relationship for anything in the world. How on earth are we going to get past this, because I know that it will be very hard for me to forget how I felt about him under that spell, it was too amazing to be forgotten. I wonder if he's thinking about the same thing right now.

My sad thoughts are interrupted as the bell rings, signaling the end of class. I think I hear practically everyone breathe a sigh of relief as they all get up to leave the classroom. This was the second to last class of the day, and I think every else shares the same feelings I have, we just want this weird day to be over. I pick up my bag and walk out the door with everyone else. I glance over to my side to see Luis leaning against the lockers, waiting for me so that we can walk to class together just like always. I smile at him, glad that he doesn't feel so weird about everything that he wouldn't walk with me.

"Hey Colomba, how was class?" The two of us start walking beside each other to head down the hall.

"It was okay, nobody was really paying attention though. I think everybody is still getting over what just happened with the Crow." Luis nods at that in understanding.

"I bet, I couldn't get it out of my mind either. Today has definitely been… eye opening." I keep silent for a moment as I try to gather up my courage to try and say what I think needs to be said between us.

"Hey Luis." I say this in almost a whisper, my embarrassment almost making me mute.

"Yes?" He responds with curiosity lighting up in his eyes.

"I'm sorry about how I was acting earlier. I was under the Flying Ace's spell and I'm sorry if I made you uncomfortable with all of that lovey-dovey stuff." He smiles at me warmly.

"It's okay, I understand. You couldn't control yourself, neither of us could." I let out a little sigh of relief.

"Oh good. I didn't want things to be all weird between us." He chuckles.

"We're good, don't worry. You know, you were actually really sweet when you were my "girlfriend"." He makes little quotation marks in the air with his fingers when he says girlfriend. This makes me chuckle a little. "I know that whoever you end up with will be the luckiest guy on earth, and you deserve to be with the best guy in the world." I smile as I give Luis a hug.

"Thanks Luis, that's so sweet of you to say. You were such a great "boyfriend" to me too. You are definitely going to make some girl very happy one day." I release him from my embrace. "Well I have to get going to my next class, I'll talk to you later Luis." He nods at me with a smile, but for some reason the smile seems a bit sad and forced. Did he lie and does he still feel weird about this, or does he feel sad about something else? I'm too afraid to ask.

"Yeah, I'll see you later." He turns away and walks down the hall, but I don't head to my next class just yet. I watch him as he walks away from me. For some reason a miserable feeling had come over me as soon as I saw that sad smile on his face, and I feel even worse now that he isn't beside me. I want to just go up and talk to him. I want to be beside him and see him smile, a real smile. It actually hurts my heart to see him so unhappy. My heart leaps a little in my chest when I realize another reason why I feel this pain. I'm sad that he isn't my "boyfriend" anymore. I am sad that we can't be like that anymore now that we're not under the Flying Ace's spell.

I look away from him, not wanting to think like that anymore. It must be some effect from the spell that hasn't worn off yet. I can't let that get the best of me. I need to just ignore these feelings. As I look back at Luis though, I don't really want to ignore what I'm feeling. I turn away from him to head to my next class. Luis is just a friend, he doesn't see me as anything else. I need to keep reminding myself of that. I need to keep doing that until this spell has completely worn off. As I think about what happened though, I don't know if I want it to wear off. I don't want to stop feeling in love with him.

Chapter Twenty
Luis-
Harsh Truth

After I had walked a little ways down the hall, I turn around so that I can watch Colomba as she walks away, wanting to say something but I am too afraid to try. My eyes follow her until she turns a corner and goes down another hallway, out of my sight. I glance over to the side to see that somebody had been watching me. Nat is looking at me sadly, and I have a feeling that she saw everything that just happened.

"What?"

"You weren't under the Flying Ace's spell, were you? I remember everything that was going on when I was under that spell. I remember how Colomba was in love with you, and you were in love with her. The thing is though that everyone that was under the spell was stuck with somebody that they would never be with in a million years, but you were with the person you have been in love with for what feels like ever. This doesn't make sense unless you just pretended that you were under the spell too and let it all go on. Did you do this to her?" I look away from Nat, knowing that I can't hide my feelings from her.

"I just wanted to be with her. It was a dream come true having her finally love me back. I guess I just couldn't handle the temptation." I feel tears beginning to form in my eyes, but that is easily forgotten when Nat rushes up to me and slaps me across the face. My inner pain is immediately forgotten at her sudden attack. I see a few people stop and stare at us, wondering why on earth I just got slapped and wanting to see whatever drama is about to happen. "*What was that for?*" Nat glares at me with pure venom, completely ignoring the small crowd of people watching us.

"If you love her than show it! Don't lie and pretend to be with her just to make yourself feel good! If you want to be with her then stick your neck out and ask her!" I look away from Nat, afraid of her anger. I have never seen Nat act like this before, it's really frightening.

"But I can't." I say this in almost a whisper, but Nat comes back in full force.

"Why not?!" I feel the tears return as I tell her the truth, I say the sad truth in a whisper that I know only she can hear, scared that the small crowd around us will hear what I have to say.

"She'd say no. She's better than me, no girl would sink so low as to be with me. Everyone treats me like dirt. What could I ever give to a girl?" Nat just rolls her eyes and groans in annoyance.

"C'mon Luis you've been saying that for almost two years now! I told you not too long after we met that a girl would be happy to be with you! You're a nice guy, and sometimes nice guys are hard to find! You're only saying that as an excuse! You always have some kind of excuse! Face it Luis, you're just saying that because you're afraid! You always have some excuse for not saying how you feel! If you want to be with her then take a chance! Get off your butt and do it!" She practically marches away from me and the small crowd parts to let her pass through, some of them looking a bit afraid of getting in her way since she looks so angry.

The people who had stopped to watch start walking away, all of them giving me one last glance of confusion before heading to their final class of the day. They all look like they want to ask me why she was so upset with me, and who we were talking about, but they can all see that I am in no mood to talk and would probably just get mad at them if they did ask. I feel completely defeated, as if my entire world is completely tearing itself apart. The girl of my dreams no longer loves me and thinks of me as just a friend, I feel guilty about making her love me like that, one of my best friends just slapped me across the face and yelled at me in front of a bunch of people, and I feel completely alone and unloved in this world. All of the people around me can see that I am in pain and let me be despite their curiosity, but apparently one person doesn't care about my feelings, and when I recognize the voice I'm not surprised that they don't care.

"Wow, that's just pathetic." I turn my head to see Alex sauntering up to me, an evil, pleased grin on his smug face. "I knew that a loser like you could never be with a girl like Colomba, but to pretend to be with her like that, that's just sad man." He chuckles while he shakes his head, Alex looks at me as if I am a disgusting bug that he plans on crushing. "Now everything just makes sense, only a spell could force Colomba to sink so low and be with a guy like you." I feel my rage boil over and I want nothing more than to punch him right across his smug face, but I hold that back and instead look him right in the eyes and say something to him that I usually would never dare to say.

"Well then of course that trashcan you were kissing must have been under that spell too, since not even a trashcan would sink so low as to be with you." Amazingly, a talkative guy like Alex has nothing to say to that, he just stares at me with open mouthed shock as I turn around and walk away from him. I should feel pretty proud of what I just did, I just stood up to Alex like I never do, but the pain is still there in my heart. I guess I deserve to feel this way. Even though I have had a small victory over Alex, I still deserve to feel the pain. My feet drag across the floor as I head to my next class as I wonder what on earth I can do next to try and fix what I have done.

I make it to class without anything else happening, the teacher starts the lesson, but I don't pay attention. My thoughts are still stuck on the problem I face with Colomba. What can I do to finally confess to Colomba about how I feel about her? Once I do that, I can finally stop all this pretending. Even if this ends badly and she rejects me, we may be able to still be friends. At least, I hope we can.

While the teacher keeps talking, I try to think of a way to ask Colomba out. I know that I can't just ask her face to face, I would be a chicken and not go through with it because I would be too scared that she will say no. Okay, so if I can't say it to her face, I need to be more clever about it. After a minute or two of thought, I still have nothing. My eyes scan the room, hoping to find some inspiration for what I can do. I see some people trying to write notes on what the teacher is saying while everyone else is either staring off into space or whispering to each other about what happened earlier with the Flying Ace and Silver Dove. I guess once super powered people have a fight in the school, it makes it hard to concentrate for the rest of the day. My eyes stop when I notice something on a girl's desk that gives me a brilliant idea.

Laying across her desk (she probably laid them there so that everyone could see it and be jealous) is a single red rose, and on that rose is a little note where the person who gave it to her wrote how much they like her and want to be with her. My mind immediately flashes to the lily that I had bought to give to Colomba this morning, but never did because I was interrupted by Alex. That's what I can do for her, I can write a note and attach it to the lily. That's brilliant, then I won't have to say anything to her face, and I won't be too embarrassed to say anything. The only question though is how will I say how I feel?

Pulling out my notebook, I start writing

down different ideas of what I can say. I write sentence after sentence, but each time I end up scribbling it out because it doesn't sound quite right. It doesn't sound perfect. This needs to be absolutely right so that she is more likely to say yes when I ask her out. I tap my pencil against my notebook as I stare at the page full of scribbled out words. Colomba has always tried to encourage me with my art, so maybe I should put some of that into this note. A sudden idea comes to me and my pencil flies across the paper as I write a poem to her. When I am done, I hold it up so that I can read it.

Your eyes are like the ocean
Your heart as boundless as the sea
I would give up everything
To have you here with me

For you, I would do anything
I would move a mountain
I would stop the hands of time
If you would just be my Valentine

It feels a little sappy, but I think that it will work. Ripping the paper out of my notebook, I put it in my pocket to make sure that I will know where it is when I need it. Before school ends today, I will need to get to my locker where I left the flower, write down this poem in the little card on the flower, and then put it on Colomba's locker before she gets there. I will need to be quick to get this right, but I think I can do it.

I stare at the clock for the rest of the class, practically begging the hands on the clock to move faster, until the bell finally rings, signaling the end of the last class of the day. Everyone picks up their bags and start chatting while I swipe my bag off the ground and run out the door. They can waste their time, but I have a mission to fulfill. I run through the halls as everyone starts heading out the doors of their classes. I almost run past my locker I was going so fast. Spinning the combination for the locker, I open it and snatch the flower out of it. Slamming the door shut, I run again, heading straight for Colomba's locker. People stare at me as I go by and I hear a few of them asking their friends why I am running so fast, but none of them would ever guess the real reason. I am running to go pour my heart out to the most amazing girl in the world.

Getting to Colomba's locker usually takes me three minutes or so, today, in my hurry, I make it in less than one. The second I make it there I am writing the poem onto the card attached to the flower. My hand seems to fly across the little piece of paper. When I am almost done, I glance around to make sure that Colomba is not close enough to see what I am doing. She is nowhere in sight, but I do not breathe a sigh of relief because I do see one person coming closer that could ruin everything, Alex. He hasn't seemed to notice me yet, which probably has saved my life since he is probably still angry about the comment, I made about him and the trashcan. I finish writing the poem as fast as I can, place the flower into one of the little holes in her locker, and then run off before Alex can see me. When I am in the next hallway, I glance around the corner to see that Alex hadn't seen me and he hasn't noticed the flower on Colomba's locker either, he passes it without a second glance. Wow, I'm actually pretty impressed by my own speed, I feel pretty good about myself right now.

Apparently, I had made it out of there just in time, because only seconds after hiding behind the corner Colomba comes around another corner and heads straight for her locker. My hands tighten into fists at my side as I anxiously wait. I see her head cock to the side in confusion and surprise when she sees the lone flower stuck on her locker. Gently, she picks up the flower and smiles, seeing that it is her favorite flower, a star gazer lily. One of her delicate little hands holds the card and starts reading the poem. Colomba smiles softly as she reads it, and I can instantly tell that she likes it, she likes it a lot. Now is my moment. Walking casually around the corner toward her, I try to seem confident even though it feels as if my insides are eating themselves, I am that scared.

"Hey Colomba." She glances up from the card to smile at me with pure joy.

"Hi Luis." She looks back down at the card.

"What are you reading?" I can see her blush a little at my question.

"Someone wrote a poem for me along with their flower." She falls silent as her face breaks out in the biggest smile I've ever seen. "Wow, this is so sweet." She flips the card over and her eyebrows lower in confusion, she examines both sides of the card closely and I'm confused as to what is confusing her. "That's strange, they wrote this poem for me, but they didn't write their name on it." My heart instantly sinks into my chest. When I was writing the poem in front of her locker, I had been in such a hurry to get away from Alex that I had forgotten to put my name on it. I have to be the most pathetic idiot in the world. Okay, you may have made that mistake, but you can just tell her now. Just say it, say that the poem is from you, tell her that you wrote it because you care so much about her, that you love her. I look down at her as she reads the poem again. As I look at her, I see an angel. I open my mouth to speak to this angel, my voice cracking as I speak.

"That is really strange, I have no idea why they did that." ***You coward!! Tell her you idiot!! Don't back down again!!***

I scream this at myself in my mind, but when I look at her, I can't. I just can't do it. I can't tell her. I can't tell her because I know how it will end; she may have loved my poem, but she doesn't love me. She will reject me and we will no longer be friends, and I will lose the one person in my life who has been a true friend to me. I can't lose her.

My heart shatters in my chest as she reads it aloud to me, and when we get on the bus, she reads it aloud again to Nat. As she reads it to Nat, Nat glances over at me curiously. I'm pretty sure that she suspects that I wrote it, but I will never tell her, she already chewed me out enough today to last me a lifetime. When the bus makes it to my stop, I walk into my Uncle Diego's shop and thankfully he is talking to a customer about some old tea set, so I rush up to our apartment upstairs so he won't be able to ask me how my day went and I won't have to try and hide my disappointment since I told him this morning that I was going to confess to Colomba and he will ask about that. I just want to be alone after this miserable day. I close the door to my room and lay down on my bed. Closing my eyes, I place my hands on my chest, trying to relax.

"Well you certainly messed up, didn't you?" I practically leap out of my bed to see Shadow perched on my bedside table, glaring at me with her black eyes. I hold back a groan when I realize what happened. I must have placed my hand on the Crow Medal when I rested my hands on my chest. I feel my body tense, just looking into her dark, enraged eyes lets me know that I'm about to get it.

"C'mon Shadow, please don't yell at me, Nat already yelled at me enough." Her feathers ruffle in her anger.

"I'm not going to yell at you, but I will say what I think. You did a terrible thing today." I close my eyes and turn away from her.

"Please Shadow-"

"Don't you "please Shadow" me." Shadow interrupts in a stern voice that instantly silences me. "You tried to force Colomba, the girl you say that you love, into loving you. Someone who is truly in love would not do something as terrible as that. She is a very kind, loving girl who has given so much to you, and this is how you repay her, by controlling her like a puppet?" I take in a deep breath, trying to control myself.

"It wasn't like that Shadow." I try to sound calm, but a trace of rage is still in my voice.

"Then explain it to me, what was it like then?" She says this with cold sarcasm that is making it harder for me to keep my anger under check.

"I just saw it as the only way I could be with her. I was never going to ever get a chance with her anyway with everything how it is normally, so why not change a few things to have her?" From the corner of my eye, I can see her shaking her head with pity. Her voice is much softer this time when she speaks in a voice like you would have when comforting a crying friend.

"Master, you must open up your eyes. Things aren't as terrible as you think. You have created a prison for yourself in your own mind by thinking so negatively about yourself. To you everything is doom and gloom, everything will always turn out bad. I know that you probably think that way because life has not been easy for you, but-" This time I don't hold back my fury, I turn back to face her, glaring at her with as much fire and venom as I can.

"***Easy?!*** It hasn't been ***easy***?! You obviously have no idea what you are talking about! It was a lot more than just "not easy"!! You don't know what it was like for me! Have you spent years at a time without a friend?! Have you cried alone at night, wondering why the world hates you and why nobody seems to care?!" I stop for a moment so that I can control myself before I start talking again. "So many things have happened to me, so many things I have never even told you about! I had all of this stuff happen and then I finally had something good happen, I met Colomba. She's one of the only good things that has happened to me. I can't lose her! I love her too much! I just wanted to be with her!" I feel the tears forming in my eyes, but Shadow surprises me with harsh words.

"Don't try to give me these excuses." Her words are practically a growl. "You took control over how she felt, there is no excuse for that! She has always been kind to you, and she considers you to be one of her best friends. Despite all of that, you betrayed her! You controlled her as if she meant nothing to you!" I look away from her before I ask her a question.

"If you could make the person you love love you back, wouldn't you do it?" Her feathers start to stick out and I can tell that she is tensing every muscle in her tiny body in her rage.

"It doesn't matter if I had the power, I wouldn't do it because it wouldn't be right. If you want to be loved, you need to do it the right way. You need to earn it. You can't control them. I hope that you can learn this one day." Shadow flies off my dresser and flies back into the medal, leaving me alone in my room.

Only when I am sure that she's gone do I finally show my true feelings. I practically fall onto my bed as my body shakes with sobs. How could I do that to her? Why? No, I can't ask myself why, because I know why, I'm pathetic. I thought that since I could never be with her, I should just force it. As I lay down on my bed in tears, a devastating thought goes through my head. Silver Dove was right, you can't make people like you. No matter how much you want to. I have wanted to be loved for years, but have only been loved by my uncle. He has been the only person to show me love and kindness, that is until I met Colomba. She made me feel special, she made me feel like I mattered in this crazy, mixed up world. She made the world seem brighter and full of life to me. I can't bear to think of the world without her, I just needed to have her with me. I needed her to love me. To have her love anyone else seems like the worst torture I could ever imagine. I guess in my pathetic mind, I would do anything to escape that torture, even control the mind of the girl I love.

I sob for what feels like hours as I think about what I have done, and I realize the monster I must be to have done something like that to someone as sweet and gentle as Colomba. She deserves better treatment than that, she deserves someone better than me, someone who wouldn't have done something like that to her. Even though I know that she deserves better than me, I still feel in my heart that I want to be with her. My heart breaks as I wonder what I need to do because I feel more lost than I have ever been in my entire life.

Chapter Twenty- One
Colomba-
A Devastating
Prophecy

My grandmother and I sit on our couch in the living room, sewing a quilt together, as I finish telling her about everything that happened today.

"It was all so weird. I still don't understand why the Crow wanted everyone to fall in love. He's never done anything like that before. The Crow usually just has someone attack the school, not make the school all lovey- dovey, I don't get it. What made him change his strategy all of a sudden?" Nonna shrugs at me as she tries to add a new patch to the quilt.

"I am not sure either, I was honestly very confused about everything you have told me. Maybe he wants to change how he does things so that he won't be seen as the villain anymore and more people will support him." I nod at her words, seeing that she has a point and that might be his plan, but something in the back of my mind tells me that that's not right.

"I don't know, I don't think that's it. Something about this doesn't seem like he was trying to do his usual take over the school and let this person have their revenge kind of thing. This felt like he really wanted people to be in love. Some of those people seem to have been chosen to be together, like Angela and the guy who's in charge of the Crow's fan club. It seems like they were planned to be together since Angela would hate it the most. It seems like a lot of the bullies in school were like that, they were either with someone they made fun of or were with a person or thing that they would hate, like Alex with the trashcan. Since I saw all that, I'm pretty sure it wasn't random. It makes me wonder if all of the couples were planned. If it was planned, then why did they pair me with Luis?" Nonna stops working on the quilt for a moment to look up at me.

"Was it so bad being with Luis?" I glance over at her, confused by her words. It almost sounds as if she is trying to point something out to me about Luis, but I'm not sure what it is?

"Not really. He was wonderful to me when we were both under the spell. He treated me like a princess and was willing to do anything to make me happy. We were both so happy just to make the other person happy." I stop working on the quilt as I try to figure out how to say what I think needs to be said. "I want to fall in love with a sweet, intelligent, fun guy. Luis would be nice to be in love with, but he just thinks of me as a friend. We aren't meant to be together I guess, he just isn't that interested. I know that I will meet the right guy for me some day, but I guess I just haven't met him yet." Nonna stops sewing as she lets out a soft sigh.

"You have already met him." My grandmother closes her eyes as if she doesn't want to look at me when she continues to speak. "Tesoro there is something that I need to tell you. I should have told you this ages ago, but I didn't want to worry you. You have said so many bad things about this person in the past, and I was hoping that your opinion of them would have changed before I told you, but now is probably the best time." There is something in her voice that makes me instantly concerned, it almost sounds as if she is about to tell me that the world is ending.

"What is it? What's wrong?" Her hands ball up into fists on the quilt we are working on, her fists are shaking, terrified of what her words will do to me. She releases a deep sigh before she speaks again.

"It is said that those who wear the medals are destined to be together." I narrow my eyes, kinda confused by what she means.

"Yes, I already know that we're supposed to be working together, you've told me that before. There's no reason to be upset by that since it's never going to happen, he's not going to get that through his head so we will just have to be enemies." Nonna shakes her head at me, pain showing in her face.

"No, not work together, be together. Those who wear the medals are destined to fall in love. It is what happened with me and your grandfather, and it has happened countless times before. It is what's going to happen with you and this new Crow." It takes me a second to realize that I heard her correctly. I feel my body recoil in shock as I stare at her in horror.

"No, no that can't be true." My voice comes out in a frightened whisper, she just nods her head at me as tears form in her eyes. She can see my pain and she feels it too. Nonna understands how I feel about the Crow, and she knows that I would be miserable knowing that I will end up with a creep like him.

"I'm sorry, but it is. Every single person who has been chosen to wear that pin has fallen in love with the person who has another like it. It has happened every time since the pins first came to be all those centuries ago. You cannot escape it Tesoro. You and the Crow are destined to be together. You will fall in love one day and you will be together for the rest of your lives." The tears fall down my face as I imagine the fate I have been given. I will fall in love with a maniac, I will end up with this terrible person who is constantly trying to hurt people. My mind flashes through all the dreams I had for my future. I've imagined ending up with a sweet guy that I can spend the rest of my life with, someone who will be supporting as I go and be a doctor and create a family together. Those dreams shatter in front of me now as the Crow's masked face invades my mind. That horrible, horrible masked face.

I feel my heart pounding with worry in my chest when I think back on a few things. When the Sprinter attacked, the Crow saved me by getting the rocks off of me and getting me to a safe place. When the Giant captured me before I transformed into Silver Dove, the Crow told the Giant to be careful with me so that I wouldn't get hurt. Does the Crow already love me as myself because of these pins, yet hates me as Silver Dove? Has the pin already worked its magic on him and made him love me?

I stare down at the pin on my sweater. Only a few minutes ago I would feel happy looking at it, but now I only feel hatred. Now, I feel like ripping it off my sweater and throwing it out the window. I want nothing more to do with it. This is what I want, but I know I can't do it. Everyone is relying on me to save them from the Crow and whoever he transforms next, they need me to save them from the villain I will end up with. I lower my head into my hands as I let myself sob uncontrollably. Nonna tries to comfort me, but there's no way that I can be comforted. I feel as if my entire world has crashed in around me. Everything I have ever dreamed of is now over. My only hope is to not fall into the power of the pin and not love him, but according to Nonna, that's impossible. Everyone who has worn the pins before have fallen in love, and the Crow and I will be next. It is only a matter of time before I start living my nightmare.

Chapter Twenty- Two
Luis-
Terrible News

Stepping into my room after dinner, I sit down at my desk to start drawing my sketch of the Flying Ace in my sketchbook full of other things for the Crow. My Uncle Diego must have noticed that I was upset, so he did not ask how things went with Colomba and I. My pencil scribbles over the page as I get started. Around fifteen minutes pass in complete silence as I sketch the Flying Ace. When I am almost at the end of the drawing, I place my hand on the Crow medal to summon Shadow. I know that she was mad at me earlier, but I feel a bit lonely and want to apologize to her for the way I have been acting today. I don't like it when she is mad at me, it almost feels as if my mother is upset with me whenever she gets like this. It is a heartbreaking feeling. Shadow appears on my desk, perched on top of a mug that I hold my drawing pencils in.

"I'm surprised, I didn't expect you to summon me any time soon. We were both very upset the last time we spoke earlier today." I lower my eyes, ashamed with myself for how I acted toward her. Shadow has always been a good friend to me, always wanting the best for me, and I shouldn't treat her like that, she deserves better.

"Yeah, I wanted to tell you that I'm sorry. I was mad and I said some things that I didn't mean to. I'm really sorry about all of this." Birds can't smile, but it almost feels as if Shadow is smiling at me right now.

"It's alright, I forgive you. You have had a very tough day. You made some mistakes, but you tried to fix them as well. I am disappointed for what you did, but I am proud that you realized your mistake and decided to end the curse you put on everyone. You did the right thing even though you would lose someone's love whom you truly care for." I feel myself blushing at her compliment, I focus on the drawing I am finishing so I won't have to look at her.

"Thanks Shadow." I hear a slight sound, I can't really tell what it is, but I realize that it was the sound of Shadow hopping off my pencil mug and landing right on top of the drawing I'm working on, obviously trying to tell me to stop so that I will listen to her. I look up to see that her face is only a few inches from mine, her black eyes staring deeply into mine.

"I do mean it, I am proud of you. When I first met you, you probably would have kept the spell over everyone so that you could stay with Colomba. Today was different though, you did the right thing even though it wasn't what you wanted.

Every day it seems to you are slowly changing from the selfish little boy I met, to a more mature man. It has been a real joy to watch you grow so much these past two years." I let out a faint sigh.

"But I still did it though, I did something unthinkable, I hurt her. I hurt the girl I love and-"

"And you stopped." Shadow interrupts. "You are always beating yourself up about something, sometimes you need to realize when you have done something good. Yes, today started off pretty badly, but you stopped what you were doing before Silver Dove could convince that Lexi girl to stop or beat her to a pulp. You did that on your own." I smile at her, realizing that she is right about that part, I did fix my mistake, but I can't be really happy as the image of Colomba's smiling face enters my mind.

"Yeah that is true, I guess, at least I did something good today." I rub my hands against my face, trying to get rid of the exhausted feeling I have. It barely helps, I still feel as if I have just carried the weight of the world on my shoulders. "I just love her so much, just seeing all those cards and gifts from other guys, and Alex acting that way around her, I just lost my mind for a little bit. I couldn't stand the thought of her being with another guy, someone who won't love her as much as I do." I look deeply into Shadow's eyes, almost pleading with her to say what I want to hear. "Do you think that Colomba and I are meant to be together? Do you think that she will ever love me too?" She doesn't say anything for a moment, she looks at me as if she is trying to make a hard decision in her head before saying her answer. Shadow apparently makes up her mind because she lets out a little sigh, and lowers her head so that I can't see her face.

"I'm sorry Master, but no. It will not happen." Her words feel like a bullet ripping through my chest. Shadow has always been the one to try and give me confidence and not beat me down. Despite all that and the kind words she was just saying to me, here she is shattering my heart.

"W-what? What do you mean? There must be at least a little bit of a chance though." Shadow just shakes her little feathered head, pity showing in her black eyes.

"You are not meant to be with her. Throughout the centuries, those who have worn the medals are destined to be together. You are destined to fall in love with Silver Dove, not Colomba. She will never be yours." I sit there, just looking at her for a moment before the reality of what she said finally kicks in.

"No, that's not true, you have to be lying to me." I say this in a whisper, as if I am begging for this to not be true. She just looks into my pleading eyes, the pity still shown in every feature of her face.

"It is true, you will fall for Silver Dove. I am sorry." Without thinking, I slam my fist into the closet door beside me. Shadow jumps a little in surprise at this, her feathers puffing out and turning her into a black ball of fluff in her fear. Seeing her fear only makes me more angry. My fists fly as I punch the door at least eight more times, in my frustration I can't keep track.

This can't be true, it just can't be. In the past two years, having Colomba be a part of my life has been the only thing I have really wanted. Now it feels that the dreams I have were just snatched right out of my hands. My heart keeps telling me that this is not true, that Shadow is wrong, but when I look into those wise eyes, I know that she wasn't lying. She was being perfectly honest with me, and I know that there is nothing I can do to stop it. It will happen.

Looking down at my hands, I can see that they are bleeding from when I had punched the door. I hadn't even felt any pain in my hands because I was feeling so much pain in my heart. As the blood starts to drip down my knuckles and onto the floor, my tears start to drip down as well. I have tried so hard to be with her, the girl I have always dreamed of, but I have already lost her. I have lost her because of the medal that I've been given, the medal I thought would help me win her. My first thought is that I should just throw this away and then that rule will not apply to me anymore, but I know that I can't. This medal is one of the few things that makes my life worth living. This medal makes me feel as if I actually have strength even though I know that I am weak. It makes me feel as if I can do anything even though I know that I still have limits. And it makes me feel as if I still have a chance in this world even though my mind always tells me that I will always be a failure.

Wait a minute… I may have a chance. This medal doesn't control me, I control it. I don't have to do what it wants, I am my own master. Walking to the other side of the room, I look out the window at the setting sun. It has turned the sky as red as the blood dripping from my hands. My eyes glare deeply at nothing, almost daring the world to get in my way. I will do whatever it takes to not fall under the spell of the medal, because I will never be with another girl besides Colomba. She is the only one I will ever love.

I practically scream this in my mind as the sun slowly falls beneath the horizon, letting my world fall into complete darkness.

Chapter Twenty- Three
Colomba-
The Dark
Flower

I stare up at the ceiling as I lay down in my bed. My body wants sleep, but my brain won't shut up and let me rest. No matter how much I want to sleep, my mind keeps reminding me of what Nonna told me earlier, I will end up with the Crow. My stomach churns, making me feel sick. I roll over so that I am looking at the lily that I put in a little vase on my bedside table. Despite my dark thoughts, looking at that beautiful flower makes me feel a little better. It makes me feel so much better looking at it and knowing that someone was kind enough, and cares for me enough, to do something so sweet for me.

I stare at the flower, the moonlight reflecting off of its pale petals. A sudden feeling of horror comes over me as a dark realization passes through my mind. The person who gave this to me… they didn't sign their name. I don't know who gave this to me. Did they not sign it on purpose? Did the person who gave it to me… is it the Crow? The Crow already seems to have a crush on me, so is it really that hard to believe that he would give me a flower? The sick feeling in my stomach just gets worse as I look at it. Suddenly I start feeling a bit afraid as I watch the moonlight dance on the flower petals.

My body shivers as I continue to look at it. Only moments ago, I thought that flower was beautiful, now I only see something to fear. Without even thinking of it, I snatch the flower out of the vase and throw it across my bedroom. The lily hits the wall opposite me and falls to the ground, one of its petals falls off from the impact and slowly falls to the ground. I stare at it in horror as the moonlight makes the broken flower look as if it is glowing in the dark, like a ghost.

I stare at it, almost as if I am daring that little flower to tell me who sent it to me. Deep down though, I think I already know the answer, but I am afraid to believe it. So even though it is late at night, and my body aches in my exhaustion, I just stare at the broken flower. I am just hoping and praying that I am wrong, that Nonna is wrong, and that I can finally find true happiness in this crazy upside-down world. As the night goes on and the city sleeps, I stay awake and pray for peace. Hours pass before my eyes finally close, and sleep takes me.

As soon as I fall asleep, my eyes pop open again to a bright, beautiful day. I recognize where I am standing. It is the flower filled courtyard that I have seen in my dreams before. This dream is different though, I am my usual self, I am Colomba not a dove. I glance around and see the fountain with the three people on it, the willow tree that the crow always stands under in my dreams, and the hundreds of flowers around me. In this dream though, I recognize something I hadn't noticed before. In one corner or the courtyard is a plant that instantly catches my eye. I walk over to it to see that many flowers just like I had been given by my secret admirer today are growing all over it. It is a beautiful sight to see, and I take in the scent of them. A smile grows on my face for a moment before I hear a faint sound behind me that instantly sends a shiver down my spine. The sound of large wings beating near me.

"I was hoping that I would see you soon." I turn around so quickly that I stumble right into the Crow. He places his hands on my shoulders and holds me so tightly that I cannot move. The Crow looks down at me, a smile forming beneath his mask. "I've been waiting for you for a long time." I reach up to try and place my hand over the Silver Dove Pin so that I can transform, but the Crow seems to know what I am planning. He grabs my hand and smiles at me as if I am a naughty child who just got caught doing something bad. "There's no need for that, my love." He lets go of my hand so that he can take the pin off my cardigan. He holds it up in front of my face, like a kid showing off a new toy. "You won't be needing this anymore. Don't worry though, I will always be here to protect you, my love." He tries to rest his hand on my face, but I slap it away from me.

"I am not your "love", and I will never be

yours." The Crow's smile is gone in an instant. He grabs my shoulders again, but much harder this time. His grip on my shoulders is so strong that I actually whimper a little because of the pain. His dark eyes glare into mine. So much anger is there that I want to scream and run away like a small child, but with his tight grip on me I know that I couldn't get away. The Crow leans in close to me so that we are practically eye to eye. He stares deeply into my eyes for a moment before whispering to me in a menacing tone.

"You will be mine someday soon, you might as well just get used to it." I open my mouth to scream, praying that somebody else will be nearby and they can help me. When the scream is about to leave my lips, I feel myself sit bolt upright in my bed. I breathe heavily for an entire minute before my heart stops racing. My mind races through everything in the dream and what the Crow said. If what Nonna said is true, then I will end up with him. If I do, will he really be like that to me? Would he be cruel to the woman he loves? And is there really nothing I can do to stop this from happening?

Even though my body is begging for sleep, I stay awake until the sun starts to bring light back into the world. I stay awake, thinking about my ruined future with a monster who loves me.

Don't miss the previous books in The Adventures of Silver Dove series.

Eliza Scalia is a therapist who has a master's degree in Clinical Mental Health from Troy University. She enjoys reading, writing, and needlework, as well as hanging out with her pet cat, Dusty. Eliza has been writing since she was in middle school and has self- published the Death's Assistant series for young adults.

www.ingramcontent.com/pod-product-compliance
Lightning Source LLC
Chambersburg PA
CBHW070513200726
48293CB00007B/2511